THE TEMPTATION TO BE HAPPY

Translated by Shaun Whiteside

ONEWORLD

A Oneworld Book

First published in North America, Great Britain and Australia
by Oneworld Publications, 2017
This paperback edition published 2018
Originally published in Italian as *La Tentazione di Essere Felici*
by Longanesi, 2015

Published & translated by arrangement with Meucci Agency – Milan

Paperback ISBN 978-1-78607-352-5
eBook ISBN 978-1-78607-188-0

Typeset by Fakenham Prepress Solutions, Fakenham, Norfolk NR21 8NN
Printed and bound in Great Britain by Clays Ltd, St Ives plc

Oneworld Publications
10 Bloomsbury Street
London WC1B 3SR
England

To those frail souls
who love without loving themselves

Chapter One

Cesare Annunziata

The ticking of the alarm clock is the only sound that keeps me company. At this time of night people are asleep. They say that the first few hours of the morning are the best time for sleep – the brain is in its REM phase, the one during which you dream, your breathing becomes irregular and your eyes move quickly from side to side. A spectacle that's anything but amusing to witness – in short, it's like finding yourself in the presence of someone possessed.

I never dream. Or rather, I have no particular memories of my dreams. Perhaps because I don't sleep much and wake up early. Or because I drink too much. Or only because I'm old and when you're old your dreams are used up. Your brain has had a whole life to come up with the strangest fantasies, and it's perfectly normal that it should lose its flair. The creative vein peaks during the life of each and every one of us and then, at a certain point, the descent inexorably arrives, and at the end of your days you're no longer even capable of imagining a sex scene. In your youth, however, that is the starting point: imagining incredible nights of passion with the showgirl of the day, your classmate or even your teacher, who had for some reason taken it into her head to fall into the arms of a callow youth with spots and bumfluff. Of course, the capacity for invention begins earlier than that, in childhood, but I believe that adolescent masturbation has a great influence on the formation of creativity.

I was very creative.

I decide to open my eyes. Sleeping is out of the question in these conditions anyway. In bed the brain goes on such strange journeys. For example, I sometimes think about my grandparents' house. I can still see it, walk round it, move from one room to the other, smell the smells coming from the kitchen, hear the creak of the door of the dresser in the dining room, or the little birds chirping on the balcony. I linger especially on the furniture, remembering each tiny detail, even the ornaments. If I close my eyelids tightly I can actually look at myself in my grandmother's mirror and see myself as a child. I know I said I don't dream any more, but I was talking about sleep. When I'm awake, on the other hand, I can still have my say.

I glance at the clock and mutter a curse beneath the sheets. I thought it was five o'clock, and in fact it's only a quarter past four in the morning. It's dark outside. In the distance a burglar alarm sounds at regular intervals, the humidity blurs the outlines of things and cats crouch under cars.

The neighbourhood is asleep; I'm ruminating.

I turn on to the other side and force myself to close my eyelids again. The truth is that in bed I can't be still for a minute; I release the energy accumulated during the day, a bit like the summer sea absorbing the heat of the day to give it back to the night. My grandmother used to say that when the body can't find rest you have to stay motionless; after a while your anatomy understands that there's no point kicking up a racket and calms down. Except that to put a plan like that into action you need self-control and patience, and I ran out of both some time ago.

I realize I'm staring at a book on the little chest of drawers beside me. I've often looked at the cover of this book, and yet now I notice details that had previously escaped me. I am overcome by a feeling of amazement, then I realize what it is: I'm reading from close up. No one in the world can do that at my age. Technology has made huge strides over the last century, and yet presbyopia remains one of the ungraspable mysteries of science. I bring my hands to my face and understand the reason for my sudden and miraculous cure: I have put on my glasses, a movement that I now perform instinctively, without thinking.

The time has come to get up. I go to the bathroom. I shouldn't tell you this, but I'm old and I do what I like. In brief, I urinate sitting down, as women do. And not because my legs won't hold me up, but because otherwise my hydrant would also water the tiles in front. There's little to be done – after a certain age that particular thingummy starts to have a life of its own. Like me (and like more or less all old people), it doesn't give a hoot about anyone who wants to explain the meaning of life to it, and does as it sees fit.

Anyone who complains about old age is a lunatic. Or rather, no: blind strikes me as more apt. Someone who can't see a few inches in front of his own nose. Because there's only one alternative and it doesn't seem desirable to me. Because having got even this far is a huge stroke of luck. But the most interesting thing is, as I was saying, that you can afford to do what you want. We old people get away with everything. An old man who steals from a supermarket is viewed with candour and compassion. If, on the other hand, it is a youth, he is treated at best as a 'rogue'. In short, at a certain point in life a world hitherto inaccessible opens up, a magical place populated by nice, thoughtful, affable people. And yet the most precious thing gained thanks to old age is respect. Moral integrity, solidarity, culture and talent are nothing compared to wrinkled skin, liver spots on the head and trembling hands. In every way I am today a respected man and, please note, that isn't to be sneezed at. Respect is a weapon that allows a man to reach a goal unattainable to many, and make of his life what he will.

My name is Cesare Annunziata. I am seventy-seven, and for seventy-two years and one hundred and eleven days I threw my life down the toilet. Then I worked out that the time had come to use the esteem I have acquired in the field to have some serious fun with it.

Chapter Two

What You Need to Know

My son is homosexual.

He knows it. I know it. And yet he's never admitted it to me.

No harm done – lots of people wait until their parents die before letting themselves go and experiencing their own sexuality to the full. Except that isn't going to work with me because I plan to go on living for a long time yet, at least ten years or so. So if Dante wants to emancipate himself, he's going to have to stop caring about yours truly. I really don't plan to die for his sexual tastes.

Chapter Three

Only One Thing Divides Us

This morning my daughter Sveva, my eldest, called me.

'Dad?'

'Hi.'

'Listen, I've got a favour to ask you…'

I shouldn't have picked up the phone. Experience teaches you precisely not to commit the same idiotic mistakes for a whole life. I have learned nothing from the past, and I carry on undaunted, acting out of instinct.

'Would you go and pick up Federico from school? I've got a hearing and I'll be running late.'

'Couldn't Diego do it?'

'No, he's busy.'

'I get it…'

'You know I wouldn't ask you if I had an alternative.'

I have brought up my children well – I can't complain. But I'm not the kind of grandfather who goes and picks up his grandchildren. The sight of those poor little old men outside school stopping cars so the children can cross the road, for example, makes me shiver. Yes, I know, they're making themselves useful rather than rotting on a sofa, and yet there's nothing I can do about it – for me a 'civic-minded grandad' is like a roll of film, a telephone box, a phone token, a video cassette, objects from a time gone by which no longer have a real function.

'And then where do I take him to?'

'To yours, or you could come to the studio. Yes, do that – please bring him here.'

Now I find myself outside school waiting for my grandson. I push back the brim of my hat and slip my hands into my pockets. I've arrived early, one of the things I've learned how to do with the advancing years. How to plan your day. Not that I've got much planning to do, God knows, but I prefer to put those few things in order.

Sveva's phone call has thrown my plans into confusion. I was supposed to be going to the barber, and this evening I have a romantic assignation with Rossana. She is a prostitute. Yes, I visit tarts, and…? I still have my desires which need to be satisfied and no one by my side to give explanations to. In any case, I've exaggerated. I don't go to prostitutes exactly, not least because it would be rather difficult trying to pick up girls by bus: my driving licence expired and I haven't renewed it. Rossana is an old friend that I met some time ago, when she was going from house to house giving medical injections. So she found herself in my sitting room as well. She came early every morning, pricked my buttocks and left without saying a word. Then she started staying for a coffee, and at last I managed to persuade her to slip under my covers. Thinking about it today, it wasn't very difficult. It was only a bit later that I worked out that the fake nurse was not thrown into ecstasies by my smile, when she exclaimed with a serious expression, 'You're a nice guy, and you're handsome too, but I've got a son to help…'

I've always liked people who are direct, and since then we've become friends. She's now just under sixty, but she still has a pair of enormous bosoms and a fine, harmonious backside. And at my age that's all you need. You mostly fall in love with defects, which make the scene more believable.

Federico appears. If people around here knew that this old man dragging his grandson around was thinking about a prostitute's breasts a moment ago, they would be scandalized and would alert the child's parents. Perhaps because an old man can't possibly want a fuck.

We get into a taxi. It's only the third time that I've picked up my grandson from school, yet Federico has told his mum that he's happy to come back with me. He says his other grandpa forces him to walk, and he gets home covered with sweat. With me, on the other hand, he comes home in a taxi. And I should hope so too! I've got a decent pension, no wedding anniversaries to celebrate and two grown-up children. I can spend my money on taxis and various Rossanas. And yet the driver is rude. It happens, unfortunately. He curses, he sounds his horn for no reason, he races and brakes at the last moment, he picks fights with pedestrians and doesn't stop at the lights. As I've said before, one of the great things about old age is that you can do what you like. So I decide to punish the man who's trying to ruin my day.

'You should drive more slowly,' I exclaim.

He doesn't even reply.

'Did you hear what I said?'

Silence.

'OK, pull over and give me your licence.'

The taxi driver turns round and gives me a puzzled look.

'I'm a retired police inspector. You're driving in an inappropriate and dangerous manner, and putting your passengers' lives at risk.'

'Inspector, sorry. Today's been a bad day. Problems at home. Forgive me. I'll slow down now.'

Federico raises his head and stares at me, and is about to open his mouth. I clutch his arm and wink.

'What problems?' I ask.

My interlocutor tilts his head for just a moment, and then gives free rein to his powerful imagination: 'My daughter was about to get married, but her husband lost his job.'

'I understand.'

As excuses go, it's a good one; nothing wrong with it at all, no illness or death of a spouse. It's more credible. When we pull up in front of Sveva's office, the man won't accept any money. Another free journey from a rude Neapolitan. Federico looks at me and laughs, and I reply with another wink of the eye. He's used to my sallies by now; last time I pretended to be a financier. I'm amusing myself – I don't do it to save money. And I have nothing against taxi drivers as a profession.

Sveva hasn't come back yet. We slip into her room, Federico lying on a little sofa, me sitting behind the desk on which the photograph of her with her husband and son is the centrepiece. I'm not very keen on Diego. He's a good man, don't get me wrong, but men who are too good are irritating – that's a simple fact. And, in fact, I think Sveva is fed up too; always frowning, always in a hurry and with her mind on her job. The opposite of me today, but perhaps very similar to the former me. I think she's an unhappy woman, but she won't talk to yours truly. Perhaps she talked to her mother. I'm not very good at listening to other people.

They say that to be a good companion you don't need to give any kind of advice. You just have to be careful to be understanding – that's all women want. I'm not capable of that. After a while I get worked up, I speak my mind and turn into a wild animal if my interlocutor of the moment doesn't listen to me and continues along his own path. It was one of the reasons for my constant arguments with Caterina, my poor wife. She just wanted someone to pour her heart out to, while after two minutes I was already full to the brim with the solution she needed. Luckily old age has come to my aid: I have worked out that for the sake of my health it's better not to listen to family problems. After all, you never solve them.

The room has a beautiful, wide window that looks out on the street, crowded with passers-by, and if there were a skyscraper opposite rather than a down-at-heel building made of volcanic stone, I could almost imagine I was in New York. Except that in American cities they don't have Spanish Quarters with alleyways that slip down from the top of the hill, crumbling buildings exchanging secrets along lines hung with drying clothes, potholed streets and cars climbing half-way across some wretched pavement between a street sign and the entrance to a church. In New York side streets don't conceal a world that loses itself in its own shadows; mildew hasn't settled on people's faces.

As I reflect on the difference between the Big Apple and Naples, I notice Sveva getting out of a black SUV and heading towards the front door. As she reaches it she stops, takes the keys out of her bag, then turns round and gets back into the car. From up here all I can see are her legs, veiled by black stockings. She leans towards the driver, perhaps saying goodbye to him, and he rests his hand on her thigh. I bring the chair to the window and bump my head against the glass. Federico stops playing with his robot friend and stares at me. I smile at him and return to the scene that is playing out in front of my eyes. Sveva gets out and slips into the building. The car sets off again.

I'm looking at the room without looking at it. Perhaps I've had a hallucination. Perhaps it was Diego, who, however – small detail – doesn't have an off-road vehicle. Maybe it was a colleague who'd given her a lift. But a colleague resting a hand on her thigh?

'Hi, Dad.'

'Hi.'

'Here's my love!' she shrieks and grips Federico under the arms before covering him with kisses.

The scene brings her mother back before my eyes. She behaved exactly the same with her children. She was too affectionate, too present, solicitous, invasive. Maybe that's why Dante's gay. I wonder if his sister knows.

'Is Dante gay?' I ask.

Sveva spins round, still holding Federico. Then she sets him down on the sofa and replies icily, 'I haven't a clue, sorry. Why don't you ask him?'

He's homosexual. And she knows.

'And anyway, what makes you think of that right now?'

'Just…How was the hearing?'

She gets even more defensive.

'Why?'

'Can't I ask you?'

'You've never taken an interest in my work. Weren't you the one who used to say that jurisprudence would ruin my life?'

'Yes, I thought so and I still do. Have you seen yourself?'

'Listen, Dad, today really isn't the day for your pointless sermons. I've got things to do!'

The truth is that my daughter has made too many wrong choices: studies, work and, last of all, husband. With all those mistakes behind you, you can't just smile and pretend everything's fine. And yet I'm certainly not someone who hits the target every time; I've done the odd stupid thing, like marrying Caterina and giving her two children. Not because of Dante and Sveva – good heavens, no – but it's just that you shouldn't have children with a woman you don't love.

'How are things with Diego?' I ask.

'All fine,' she says carelessly, taking the file out of her bag and setting it on the desk. On the front page it says: *Sarnataro v. Condominium, via Roma.*

I don't understand how you can decide on your own initiative to spend your days on pointless rows, as if there weren't already enough arguments in life without adding a few more. And yet Sveva likes it. Or perhaps she forces herself to like it, just as her mother did. Caterina could draw the positive side out of every experience, while I have never been content merely to dig a bit of beauty out of all the ugliness.

'Why so many questions today?'

'It's just that we never talk…'

But she's already in the corridor, her heels echoing rapidly between the rooms and her voice immersed in a hasty conversation with a colleague. They are talking about a criminal case. Yet again, what a bore!

I watch my grandson amusing himself with some kind of dragon and I smile. Basically we're the same, the two of us, with no responsibility and nothing to do but play. Federico plays with dragons; I play with Rossana and some other trifles. Only one thing divides us: he still has a life ahead of him, and a thousand plans; I have just a few years, and many regrets.

Chapter Four

The Cat Lady

As soon as I emerge from the lift I see Eleonora holding in her arms a cat that I have never seen before. The front door is wide open, and the miasma from her flat has already spread all over the landing. I don't know how she manages not to notice, and above all how she can spend her life enveloped in that revolting stench. Eleonora is one of those old ladies you meet in the street with their little paper plate of cat food, crouching among the parked cars, and her house is now a hospice for cats in difficulties. In reality, the few cats I know I've always seen in great form, but since she maintains that she's obliged to bring them home because they're sick or injured, I prefer not to get involved. The fact is that often one of her cats, in turn, tries to escape back to freedom, far from its jailer's egoistic love.

Sometimes I just have to set a foot inside the hallway of our block to know that a few floors up Eleonora has her front door open. Obviously with so many floors available to accommodate a crazed old widow in need of love, that particular honour had to go to mine.

I still have an expression of disgust on my face as she greets me affectionately.

'Hi, Eleonora,' I reply, and try to find my keys in my coat pocket.

I'm trying not to breathe, and my life depends on how much time it takes to get out my key ring and slip into the house. At my age I can only survive a few seconds without breathing. Unfortunately, however, the thing I was hoping wouldn't happen happens: Eleonora talks to me, and I am obliged to inhale some air to reply.

'This one is Gigio,' she says with a smile, showing me the feline, which looks at least as disturbed as I am.

I frown, trying to expel the fetid effluvium from my nostrils, and reply, 'A new guest?'

'Yes,' she replies straight away, 'the latest arrival. Poor little thing, he was attacked by a dog that was about to kill him! I've saved him from certain death.'

For a moment I study the cat, which is staring placidly at the horizon, and wonder if it is already working out a plan of escape.

The next moment, a couple in their fifties, she with dyed hair and lipstick, he bald and with thick glasses that are slipping off his nose, emerge from Eleonora's flat and greet me before taking my neighbour's hand and shaking it warmly. She, however, returns neither the greeting nor the handshake.

Clearly the couple are making an effort to smile and be nice, but in fact they are horrified by the spectacle that has just etched itself on to their pupils. They sneak into the lift with one last fearful glance at the landing and at yours truly, perhaps wondering how I can be a friend of the cat lady and, more importantly, her neighbour. And yet I'm the one who is most surprised; in many years I have never seen anyone leaving Eleonora Vitagliano's flat, except her husband, a lifetime ago. Never, above all, young or at least relatively youthful individuals. Never anyone who pulled a face at the stench. And in that respect even this couple were no different.

'Who were they?' I ask curiously once they have disappeared.

To my knowledge Eleonora has no one to look after her. Certainly she has no children, her husband died some time ago, and I've never seen any relatives.

'What?' she says.

Eleonora Vitagliano is even older than me and deaf as a post, so that on the few occasions when we have to speak, I am forced to reformulate my sentences and progressively increase the volume of my voice.

'I wanted to know who those two people were,' I repeat.

'Ah,' she says, letting go of the cat, which slips into the flat and disappears down the corridor. 'They are the lady and gentleman who have come to see the house.'

'Why? Are you selling it?'

Eleonora looks at me hesitantly. Her hair is tangled, her moustache is white and her bluish hands, ridged with veins and eroded by rheumatism, look like claws.

'Have you decided to leave?' I am obliged to repeat, raising my voice once more.

'No, no. And where would I go? This is my house. This is where I want to die. I have no intention of leaving.'

I look at her curiously, and she goes on.

'My niece, my brother's daughter, do you know her?'

I shake my head.

'She's my only remaining relative. And, to cut a long story short, she is pushing me to sell. She says she's in difficulties, that the flat would go to her one day anyway and I would stay here even so, and that the house would be sold after my death. I didn't understand a word, but I nodded – I have no time to waste arguing with my family, and in any case I'm not going to sign anything. In fact, when someone comes to see the house I'll show them a complete mess.'

I have no difficulty believing what she says. Eleonora, although very old and short of a marble or two, can still command respect.

'Your niece would want to sell the empty property,' I announce, attempting to explain more clearly what we are talking about. 'The house might be a crazy place now, but the new owners could only live there after you died.'

'Yes, of course. I think I've grasped that much. I'm certainly not going to be able to live here knowing that there's someone out there waiting for me to kick the bucket, apart from my niece.'

I smile, amused, even if the behaviour of that phantom niece isn't terribly funny. If she were here, I would give her an earful.

'And you'd rather have people wandering about in your house than tell your niece the truth?' I ask, and regret it a moment later. Not so much because of the rather invasive question as because I am helping to extend the conversation unnecessarily, and thus the time during which her door remains open. It will take days to air the whole building. Luckily I haven't yet opened my own door.

'Hey, Cesare, what do you want me to say? You're right, but you know how it is? I don't want to make an enemy of her. I've lived on my own for so long and I don't need much in the way of help, but you never know how things are going to change from one day to the next. I might need her every now and again. You're on your own as well – you can understand me...' she replies and goes on staring at me.

I just say 'Yes', even though part of me wants to use a more appropriate phrase, to show her that I'm on her side.

'You have to make compromises in life,' Eleonora goes on, now gripped by the discussion, 'and old age, my dear Cesare, is one continuous compromise.'

'Yes,' I reply, as if I didn't know any other words.

For seventy years I have been the master of compromises, my dear cat lady, then I lost everything and found myself, paradoxically, free. The truth is that I had nothing more to barter, and that was my good luck. That is what I should reply, but God alone knows where it would take the debate, and the oxygen at my disposal is running out. So I say goodbye to Eleonora and slip the key into the lock just as the third door on the landing opens. A couple have been renting the flat for some months: she looks about thirty; he a little older. Both young, though, and childless, which makes them entirely out of place both in this condominium, mostly made up of old people and families, and in the world. I bet the poor things are constantly forced to give explanations for the lack of a baby in their lives – a question which, judging by her curious glance, the cat lady would also like to ask.

'Hello,' says the girl, immediately frowning at the stench.

I let out a little chuckle, and the young woman glares at me irritably.

'Hello,' I hastily reply, but she has already turned her back.

'Hello,' Eleonora exclaims, adding immediately, 'excuse me, I wonder if I might tell you that if by any chance you've seen a black cat it's mine. You know what he's like – he got used to slipping through your window via the ledge when the other tenants were living there, and I wouldn't like him to do the same thing now.'

'No. No cat. Don't worry,' the girl replies before hurling herself into the lift.

'Strange couple,' Eleonora observes.

'Why?'

'Well, they've been here for a while, but never a smile. Always "good morning" and "good evening", but they never stop to chat.'

'Well, they're kids – they're bound to have their own friendships. The important thing is that they don't cause any trouble. I wouldn't mind if they didn't even say hello to me and didn't have a name,' I reply and apply myself once more to my lock.

'His I don't know, but she's called Emma.'

'Emma...' I repeat and quickly turn round.

'Yes, Emma. Why?'

'No. Nothing. Lovely name.'

'What?'

'I said, Emma's a lovely name.'

'Oh, yes, not bad.'

'Right, Eleonora, I'll have to leave you,' I exclaim and open the door. 'If you need anything, you know where to find me.'

'Cesare?'

'Yes?'

'Can I call you if anyone else wants to see the house? The estate agent is phoning me every two minutes to give me advice I don't want.'

You see, you try to be nice and you find yourself embroiled in things that are none of your business.

'What does he want?'

'What he wants?' she says. 'The other evening he told me without much beating around the bush that I should tidy up the flat a little or else potential buyers will be discouraged. Of course, I couldn't tell him that was exactly my intention.' And she smiles.

'I see. And why wasn't he there today as well?'

'He's been and gone again, but he'll show up again in a few days' time, you'll see. If you were there it would be different. It's always different if a man's there. He wouldn't dare mention the condition of the house. If he does it again

I'll be forced to throw him out, and then what's my niece going to say?'

'OK, call me.'

'Thank you.'

I close the door behind me and sniff the air in the hallway to reassure myself that the stench hasn't invaded my house as well. Only then do I slip off my coat and go into the kitchen, shaking my head with disapproval. The fact is that I've really grown too old to allow a name to ruin my day.

Even if Emma isn't just any old name.

Chapter Five

Two Circus Performers

Rossana deserves a different life. In the sense that she should be happier, while instead she seems to be missing tricks. Perhaps because she spends her days bringing joy to her customers, and there isn't much left for her. People who make other people happy deserve gratitude and respect. Even a prostitute. Even Rossana. If she didn't exist, I would be a worse person, more nervous, perhaps a little more solitary, certainly more repressed.

Each person in a normal couple plays their own part, offers their partner what they can, however little or however much they have. Yet no one ever gives anything to Rossana – nothing except money. But money doesn't buy you care and attention.

'So, why don't we go out for a bite to eat one evening?'

I've been seeing Rossana for two years and the place furthest from the bed where we've exchanged a word has been the kitchen. I know her stretch marks much better than her taste in food, I could connect her moles like the dots in a puzzle magazine, and I don't even know if she has a sister. She mentioned her son one evening when I turned up with a five-euro bottle of Prosecco bought in a hovel behind her house. She talked and I drank; she drank and I stared at the ceiling. I've never been much of a talker.

'To eat?'

'Well, yes. In a restaurant.'

'What's happened, Mr Annunziata? Is there something you need to ask me?'

No one trusts me, that's the truth – not even my children, not even a prostitute. And yet I don't think I seem devious. Yes, perhaps, as Caterina said, I concentrate on myself a bit too much, but that doesn't mean I like deceiving my fellow man.

'Why? Can't I invite you out to dinner without a hidden purpose?'

'Hmm. I've known you for too long. Try it on with someone who hasn't met you!'

There's nothing to be done – I give up. Over the past few years I've been so busy giving out a negative image of myself that there's now no turning back. I'll die a cynic and a grump.

'We could go to a nice little place and eat fish and drink wine and talk about us for a while. Basically, we've known each other for a long time, but I don't know anything about you.'

Rossana is standing with her back to me; I'm still lying on the bed with a glass of wine in my hand, studying the old harridan's bottom. She has paused with her knickers in her hand – the suggestion must have been so shocking that it prevented her from performing so simple an action as putting on a pair of pants.

'So, what do you think? Do you like my little plan?'

Her sole response is to sit on the edge of the bed and lower her head. I go on looking at her back, and the problem is that I can no longer see her bottom. I'm aware that you have to be careful with words. It's like a crossword puzzle: one word out of place can create chaos.

'OK, if you don't feel like it it's not a problem. I'm not at all offended.'

Rossana doesn't turn round and silence falls in the room, allowing my angry gut to steal the scene with a series of loud rumbles. I go into a fake coughing fit to drown out the noise, but in reality, if I could, I would let rip a loud fart which would sort everything out straight away. I set the empty glass down on the bedside table and sit up. It seems clear to me that I've said something wrong; the problem is working out what. The fact is that I've lost my edge with women. Caterina died five years ago. I still remember my last lover, with her black pubic hair. And Rossana – well, I didn't have to make much of an effort to conquer her. It's the well-known negative side of what happens when you've been with a prostitute for too long: you forget the preambles, the preliminaries, good manners, kindness, all the things you need to get a 'normal' woman into bed.

I light a cigarette and covertly notice a tear falling down her face, before she manages to wipe it furiously away. Goodness, the last woman I saw crying was that colleague of mine – what was her name? – who told me she wanted to get serious with me. I wiped her eyes and hightailed it out of there. No, in fact, she wasn't the last one. Caterina was the last one. Except that she wept not for me, but for her ailing body. And yet even then I was only able to intervene with pointless, artificial gestures. Sometimes I start awake at night and I still think she's by my side, and then I whisper to the cold wall what I should have said to her: 'You're not alone. I'm here.'

I told her I didn't love her, but not a day goes by when I don't ask forgiveness for what I did.

'I'm sorry...' Rossana whispers.

I slide over to her and put a hand on her shoulder. Her

skin is cold and covered with little spots, and yet a few minutes ago it seemed as velvety and scented as a virgin's. In such moments I'm capable of seeing what I want to see.

'It's just that it's so many years since anyone asked me out to dinner.'

'Well, if this is the effect it has I'll withdraw the suggestion straight away!'

She smiles and wipes her eyes with the back of her hand.

'It's silly of me. I wasn't expecting it. And anyway I'm going through a difficult time right now.'

There, we've got to the nub. Now I should get up, put on my trousers, leave the money and disappear. She's a prostitute; I'm a client. Our relationship should end there, with mutual satisfaction. But with a woman, even when you're paying, if you spend too much time in her bed things get bloody complicated. So I'm obliged to formulate the question that she is silently waiting for: 'Has something happened? Do you want to talk about it?'

'Come off it. I don't want to bother you with my problems – you've got enough of your own. And besides, you come here to relax, not to listen to other people's troubles.'

That's right: I come here to relax, I pay and I don't want to hear anybody's problems. Quite right. But, who knows why, this evening I'm curious about Rossana's difficulties. And I haven't listened to anyone's problems for ages.

'Why don't we do it like this?' I say. 'We get up, we go into the kitchen, you make me an omelette and we talk about it.'

She turns round and shows me her face, now smeared with running make-up. She looks like a carnival mask, but not the kind that would make you laugh. I'm forced to shift my gaze to her pendulous breasts to remind me what I'm doing here. Then I look up again and find myself staring at my own image reflected in the mirror. Sitting on the bed

– with my belly resting on my crotch, my arms flabby, my pectoral muscles that look like a cocker spaniel's ears and the white hairs on my chest – I find myself disgusting. Yes, really disgusting. Then I turn round and find Rossana's eyes staring into mine: she's noticed my rapid eye movement, and she's smiling.

'Maybe I should change the mirror,' she remarks.

'Yes,' I reply, 'I think you should.'

When we get up, the mirror goes back to reflecting only the unmade bed. The two circus performers have finished their sad spectacle, at least for today.

Without her make-up and in her dressing gown, Rossana wouldn't bring home ten euros, but basically all she needs is some decent lingerie to sort things out.

'At your age you ought to eat a bit better,' she says.

'Yes, it's true, but cooking is one of the few things that you should do for other people, not for yourself.'

She smiles. It's as if everything I say puts her in a good mood. I don't think I'm particularly nice, and yet she makes me feel even sociable. It's a particularly admirable quality of hers (apart from her knockers, obviously). Rossana makes you think you're a better man. Maybe she's pretending, but even if she is, dear Christ, she's a great actress.

'But you've got a family? You've got kids? You never told me about that! I just know you've been married.'

It's the table we're sitting at that has given her the courage to ask me. And, in fact, sharing a kitchen is much more intimate than sharing a bed.

'Yes, I've got two children,' I stammer as I chew on a slice of bread.

My reply is frosty, and yet she doesn't let it go.

'Two boys?'

'Weren't we supposed to be talking about your problem?'

'OK, forget it.'

'One male and one female. Or maybe I should say two females.'

'In what sense?'

'The male one is homosexual,' I reply nonchalantly, and bring the glass to my lips.

This time Rossana doesn't just smile, she actually laughs.

'What is it?'

'You're talking as if he wasn't your son!'

'And am I supposed to apologize?'

'Has he got a partner?'

'Yes. In fact, he hides him from me.'

She gets up and takes the pack of cigarettes from the shelf above the sink. I take advantage of the action to ask for one, even though I shouldn't smoke – I had a heart attack three years ago. Too frantic a life, the doctors said. Smoking, drinking, not enough sleep, bad diet. For a few months Sveva kept me at her place, on a strict regime, and woe betide me if she saw me deviating from it, then I got fed up with being my daughter's son and went home to my flat, where I resumed my life as before. In any case, at my age a heart attack isn't the worst way to go.

'My son lost his job,' Rossana says after a while.

I take a drag and watch the smoke dispersing under the yellowish light of the little chandelier. The room is dark, the furniture is shabby and the tiles are cracked. In short, it's a depressing environment. But at least it seems clean.

'He has three children and a wife to keep and he doesn't know how to do it. And he won't take money from me – he won't take a thing!'

Rossana is a gentle woman, in spite of her aggressive face, her hard features, black shark-ish eyes, aquiline nose and fleshy mouth. It's precisely that contradiction that makes her so attractive.

'He doesn't actually talk to me. When I go to see my grandchildren, he takes them and goes out. He won't forgive me for what I do.'

'Why did you tell him?'

'He found out all by himself, not that long ago. Since then he doesn't talk to me.'

'Why, though? How long have you been doing it for?'

'Thirty years, a whole life!'

Good God, if she'd paid her pension contributions she'd have been able to retire soon. I try not to think about how many men have passed through this kitchen over the past thirty years and concentrate on her words. Not least because, as she speaks, I've already set my brain in motion in search of a solution.

'His employer chucked him out all of a sudden one day, without even paying him off.'

'How is that possible?'

'He was working on the black – you know how things are here.'

I do know, but I can't get used to it. She starts articulating words again, and I start pouring wine into the glass. I've stopped listening to her; an idea has just come to me.

'Perhaps there's one thing we could do,' I interrupt.

She stares at me with a half-smile, trying to guess if I'm serious or joking.

'You should ask your son if he has any proof that he's worked there, and whether anyone's willing to give evidence. He might be able to bring a good case against the man.'

'Really?' she says, her eyes lighting up.

'I said maybe…'

'How's that, then?'

'OK, trust me. You tell me the name of his employer and see if you can find any evidence that your son worked there.'

She holds her hand out towards mine, but I instinctively draw back, before I'm gripped by a kind of remorse. But Rossana has already returned to the topic we were talking about.

'What did you do for a living? Were you a lawyer or something?'

Now it's my turn to laugh. 'Excuse me. My daughter's a lawyer. I'm a quick-change artist!'

'A quick-change artist? What's one of those?'

'A quick-change artist is someone who's very good at disguises. A chameleon.'

She gives me a bewildered look before she replies: 'You'd be solving quite a big problem for me. It's all I think about all day!'

'I didn't say the situation would definitely be resolved, but I'll talk to my daughter Sveva about it. Heavens above, all she does in life is argue with other people! You'll see, your son will get his job back, or at least what he's entitled to.'

Her hand rests on my arm. This time I can't pull back – it would be too much.

'And why are you doing this for me? Why are you helping my son? Why are you inviting me to dinner?'

Too many questions make me nervous, particularly when I don't know the answers. I don't know why I wanted to help her, but suddenly it seems like the right thing to do. I get up without a word and head towards the bedroom to get my clothes.

She appears in the doorway and observes me in silence for a while, then she comes out with another question: 'Does your proposition still apply?'

'Which one?' I reply, looking vaguely at the clothes scattered around the room.

'That invitation to dinner.'

In fact, I no longer have any great desire for it. Perhaps because I've just devoured a three-egg omelette, or because at this time of night most old people are snoring peacefully in bed, but having dinner with Rossana and talking about Dante and Sveva no longer strikes me as all that fascinating. But now it's too late to turn back.

'Of course,' I reply, and struggle to bend down and pick up my socks from the floor.

Rossana comes over and hugs me from behind. The enormous weight of her chest makes me stumble, and for a moment I'm afraid I'm going to end up on the floor with my bones shattered, then I manage to straighten up and regain control.

It's the first time she's put her arms around me, but then again it's also the first time that I've eaten at her house and told her about my children. The situation is getting out of hand. I turn round in the hope that she will understand and go away, but she doesn't budge. We stay there hugging, faces a few inches apart, like a pair of teenagers on a bench outside school. She stares into my eyes; I at her chest. If I looked up, the most natural thing to do would be to kiss her. But an old man like me can't kiss a woman. There's a limit to everything.

Luckily Rossana is a worldly woman – she knows when the time has come to break a spell. She has realized that I'm staring at her bosom, and comes out with the best question of the evening: 'So, shall we have another go?'

I think about it for a moment and nod seriously. In reality, I think my thing down there doesn't really agree: keeping in training is one thing, but overworking the engine isn't such a great idea. But I wouldn't admit it even to Rossana. Then I reply, 'OK, but first take a blanket and cover up that mirror!'

Chapter Six

Soya Burgers

'Dad, open up. It's me!'

I push the button on the speakerphone and stare at the white wall, trying to give myself an answer to the question I'm puzzling over: what's my son doing here? At this unusual time of day? Luckily I don't have to, because when I open the door he's already on the landing with two shopping bags in his hand.

'Woah,' I say. 'What are you doing here?'

Dante doesn't reply; he closes the lift door with one foot, smiles and strolls past me straight into the house, or more precisely, into the kitchen. I walk behind him uncomprehendingly, waiting for an explanation.

He sets the bags down on the table and smiles at me. It's only now that I notice his clothes. He's wearing tight beige trousers, some kind of studded black boots and a shirt the colour of salmon or coral, the shade I've only ever seen on old aunts or painted on the kind of pointless knick-knacks those same old aunts fill their houses with.

'I had a job to do not far from here, and I thought I'd get you something from the supermarket downstairs. That way you don't need to carry the bags.'

'They do home deliveries' is the only phrase that comes out of my mouth, and as soon as I say it I feel like a dick.

Luckily Dante doesn't seem to notice. He rolls up his shirt-sleeves and starts getting the goods out of the bags.

'So, how are you? Any news?'

'Nothing new,' I stammer as I watch him fill the table with products, most of which I don't use.

'I didn't know what you needed, so I bought a bit of every-thing,' he goes on as if nothing was wrong.

If there's one positive thing about my son's visits it's that I never have to pretend around him – I can just be the bad-tempered sod that I've always been. Dante, in spite of my evident sociopathy, goes his own way and doesn't care what I do or say in his presence. It's as if he's developed a kind of armour so that every phrase of mine bounces off him and comes back to me.

'How's your sister? Have you heard from her?'

This time he replies with a crisp 'no' that allows no further questions. By now I should know that the only thing Dante can't bear is anyone talking to him about his sister. 'Why are you always asking about her? Pick up the phone and call her!' That's his usual answer. Or at least it has been for years. Recently, however, he seems resigned, and answers with a simple monosyllable. He's worked out that changing an old man's habits is a pretty arduous business. I've been asking him about Sveva for ever, and I wouldn't be able not to. In fact, I don't really want to know about my daughter, who calls me assiduously, but I don't really know what to say to Dante, so it seems natural for me to talk about Sveva. There's always been her between the two of us; her presence is pressing, even in her absence.

'I've bought you some diet foods, some iodine-free salt, rice mayonnaise…' he goes on as he piles tins of tomatoes on top of one another.

'I'll be eating those for a year,' I say and watch him finish the operation in silence.

At last, he turns round and says, 'I can see you're on great form!'

'You're on good form too,' I force myself to reply, trying not to look at his shirt.

Luckily the time at his disposal to take care of his poor old lonely father is already over.

'Fine, I'll be off. Speak this evening or tomorrow!' he exclaims and rests a hand on my shoulder.

At this point an exemplary father would draw his son to him and hug him vigorously, before telling him he is his pride and joy. But, quite apart from the fact that such scenes only happen in American films, I'm a long way from being an exemplary father, so he too remains fixed to the spot.

Turning round, he notices the pack of cigarettes on the mantelpiece. His expression changes immediately. 'What are you doing with those?' he asks.

'With what?' I pretend not to have understood to try to gain some time to come up with a plausible excuse.

Since the heart attack, I haven't smoked in front of my children, precisely to avoid the lecture that's bound to come unless I can find a good way out.

'They're Marino's,' I say suddenly. 'For when he comes up to see me.'

'Didn't you say he never left his flat?'

Dante has one serious defect: he remembers everything you tell him.

'Yes, he doesn't go out into the street any more, but he can climb a flight of stairs.'

He seems to believe the brazen lie, but then he says, 'Don't talk nonsense, Dad, please. I'm not a kid.'

'Oh come on…' I say, walking him towards the door.

'Now, about Saturday…' Dante begins, but the lift which has just arrived at my floor disgorges Emma, who doesn't seem very happy about encountering us, says a hasty hello and closes her front door behind her.

'Pretty neighbour you've got!' my son exclaims, leaving me rather perplexed. It's the first time he's made a remark about a woman in my presence. For a very brief moment I almost doubt his homosexuality, but then my eye falls on his coral-coloured shirt again, and I realize there can be no uncertainty. And of course a gay man can find a woman attractive. And this woman, Emma, is certainly that.

'Although she doesn't seem very nice.'

I grimace to indicate that I don't greatly care whether my neighbour is nice or not, and he says goodbye and slips inside the cabin.

'One last thing…' I say.

Dante pauses and looks at me.

'Next time you treat me like an old imbecile who needs looking after, I'm not opening the door to you!'

He bursts out laughing and presses the button.

Dante is really handsome when he laughs. And luckily he does it a lot.

The truth is, I've always preferred Sveva, but right now I couldn't really say why.

I ring the bell and hear Emma's heels approaching the door. Then the spyhole darkens and I realize that the girl is staring at my face. So I smile and say, 'Hi. It's Mr Annunziata, your neighbour.'

She opens the door and smiles politely. But in spite of her good manners it's clear that she isn't at all happy with my being there. Perhaps she thinks I'm one of those tiresome old men who are constantly trying to catch other people's attention, accosting her before taking advantage of her goodwill.

Calm down, dear. I have no intention of forcing a friendship with you and your husband. I couldn't bear your invitations to dinner, your concern and your pious expressions. I just have to get these things off my chest, that's all, and then we can go back to saying 'hello' and 'good evening' as far as I'm concerned. That's what I'd like to say to her.

Instead I say: 'My son has brought me some diet and organic products that I don't use. In my day we didn't have any of this stuff.' I take a box of soya burgers out of the bag. 'I've always eaten hamburgers made of beef, and I'm still around,' I go on with a smile, 'so I'm not going to start worrying about my health now. I thought you might be able to use these things…'

This time Emma gives a genuine smile and takes the bag that I hand to her.

'That's very kind of you,' she says.

'I could have knocked on Eleonora's door,' I add, nodding towards the closed door beside us, 'but I don't think she'd know how to cook these peculiar objects.'

She smiles at me again. I must say that my son, in spite of everything, has an eye; she's really quite special, with smooth, dark hair that falls softly to her shoulders, her figure small but well proportioned, oriental eyes and full lips. And she has one defect that adds originality to her beauty: a broken incisor that gives her an aggressive, sensual touch. If I were half the age I am, I might waste some of my time chatting her up.

'Was that your son?' she asks.

'Yes,' I reply, then gauge her expression to work out if she's worked it out – if a glance was enough to realize that Dante is gay.

'I've got a pot on the gas,' Emma says and distracts me from my absurd thoughts.

'Off you go, off you go,' I reply, and leave with a wave of the hand.

A moment later I'm back on my landing. From the corner of my eye I notice a movement behind Eleonora's door. Signora Vitagliano was engaging in one of her favourite activities: espionage.

'Old fools,' I murmur to myself as I go back into my flat. 'Glued to your spyholes, watching the world go by.'

I like excluding myself. It makes me feel different.

Definitely better.

Chapter Seven

I Was Born Sweet and I Will Die Grumpy

I've got this feeling that my neighbour, Emma, is being abused by her partner. Or her husband. Either way, that dick she lives with.

I'm old, and old people are creatures of habit – they don't like novelties. That's why they always think things are getting worse rather than better, something that takes shape over the years. So when the young couple arrived here, I turned my nose up; I thought they would disturb my peace, organize banquets, dinners, birthday parties and all sorts of things. At their age any excuse is good enough to party, and birthdays are still seen as a goal to be put behind you straight away so that you can head for the next one. At their age they still haven't worked out that yes, it's important to reach your target, but there's no rush, there's no record to beat. It's better to reach the finishing line slowly, enjoy the landscape, maintain a measured pace and regular breathing for the whole journey, finishing the race as late as possible. Because – but I don't know if young people are aware of this – once you've crossed the line no one's going to come and pin a medal to your chest.

But I was wrong: not a single party, no guests for dinner, no birthdays. The couple next door were as quiet as the grave; never a word out of place; the TV was never on too loud; no stinking bag of rubbish was ever left outside the door. An invisible couple, you might say.

Until today.

Before them there was a little family made up of wife, husband and three young children. It was hell: the little pests cried uninterruptedly for four years, the worst of my life. Being the neighbour of a family that pops out a new baby every year was a disaster: like becoming a father for a second time, or rather, taking Sveva and Dante into account, a third, a fourth and a fifth time. The real disaster was that their bedroom was adjacent to mine. I live in Vomero, a hilly part of Naples where the air is quite clean and it's cool in the summer. However, there's a problem, a big problem. My building went up in the 1960s, during the economic boom, with little accuracy and a lot of superficiality. In short, the walls only separate – they don't isolate. You're constantly sharing with your neighbours: the crying of the children next door, the peeing and flushing of the lady upstairs, a coughing fit from Marino, the old (the word is appropriate) friend who's under my feet. Here, if you're a light sleeper, even a burp two floors up can wake you.

After the first three sleepless nights I grabbed my pillow and moved to the sofa. Then one day my kind neighbours invited me to dinner, perhaps because they thought I was an old man on his own and in need of help. It's true that I'm on my own, but I don't need anybody's help. In any case, I was obliged to say yes and spend an evening in the company of those absolute pains who had robbed me of my sleep. They thought my heart would be softened by the sight of those little creatures, that I was one of those stupid old men who, to keep from thinking of death, attach themselves to those who have a future ahead of them. All in all, they hoped that my heart was less rough. They were mistaken. Generally speaking, it is said that time sweetens the character, particularly where men are concerned. Many strict fathers turn into affectionate grandfathers. The opposite happened to me: I was born sweet and will die grumpy.

But I realize I've strayed from the subject. I was talking about the new neighbours, and the fact that he, as far as I can tell, hits her. As I've said, I don't sleep much, and I sleep badly. The other night I was tossing about under the covers when the two of them started arguing. At first all that could be heard was her raised voice, then, at some point, he started shouting as well. After a while I heard a thump, as if a heavy object had fallen to the ground, then silence. My curiosity was roused, and I put my ear to the wall. I don't think I'm mistaken in saying that she was crying and he was consoling her. The next morning, while I was opening my mailbox, Emma turned up. She was wearing dark glasses and looking at the floor. As soon as she saw me she turned round and climbed the stairs.

'Hello,' I said, but she was already far away.

I was sure she had a swollen black eye, so once I reached our floor I thought I would knock on the door to check that everything was all right. I reached for the bell, then changed my mind at the last moment. I've always minded my own business and that seems fine to me, so why poke my nose into things that don't concern me? After all, my neighbour is an adult, she's a grown-up: if her husband thumps her she's free to leave. I forgot all about it until, this morning, I found the girl standing on the landing with her back to me, turning her bag upside down looking for her keys. She replied to my greeting with a hurried smile that didn't allow her to hide her swollen, bruised lip.

It's true I'm an old curmudgeon, and if one of my children ever had the courage to stand up on that thing where you deliver homilies, and launch off on a list of my best qualities, I don't think they'd be able to call me a sociable fellow. I don't hate people, it's just that I'm too caught up with myself to attend to anyone else. Even Caterina always said the same thing: 'You're not bad, you're just an egoist.' I've never agreed with that. An egoist is someone who pursues his own well-being at all costs, whereas I've never attained well-being. I've even failed as an egoist.

But we were talking about my neighbour. Violence against women is one of those topics you hear about on the news, something remote from us 'ordinary folk'. A bit like murder. It's unlikely that one of my acquaintances is going to be murdered; it's more likely that they'll be struck by lightning while adjusting their satellite dish.

In short, this woman is really starting to annoy me, because this time I can't pretend nothing is happening, particularly if she insists on strolling around the place with her face all swollen. That's why I've decided to intervene, even though I don't yet know how.

I think I'll talk to Marino – he might come up with something.

Even if it's more likely that the sun won't rise tomorrow.

Chapter Eight

The Things Not Done

Marino is one of those old pains whose grandchildren take the mick out of him something rotten, who's always repeating the same things, who can't hear, doesn't understand young people's language and doesn't know how to use a computer. But unlike many of his contemporaries he does have a computer, and very fine it looks on the desk in his study. I've always wondered what it was for, given that a typewriter is a leap in the dark as far as he is concerned, but then I discovered that it belongs to his grandson Orazio, who often goes and studies there in the afternoon.

Marino is past eighty, his breath stinks, his dentures mangle just about every syllable and sometimes he even pees himself. A disaster. And yet he's a very good person, and he's company. Admittedly he won't have you splitting your sides, but he's someone you can talk to, who listens even if he can't hear, and sometimes he even gives good advice. In my life Marino is a figure half-way between a therapist with whom I pull apart my anxieties and a priest in whom I confide my sins. The great thing is that I've never been able to stand either of them, priests or psychologists.

'And what if he works out that we were the ones who sent

the letter? What if he traces the handwriting?' Marino asks agitatedly.

I snort. I forgot to add that Marino is also a very anxious individual, and that anxious individuals make you anxious. So sometimes you end up with this vicious circle that generates attention without any real reason for it and, above all, you can't tell who was responsible for it in the first place.

'Apart from the fact that I don't think the secret services would go out of their way over a message from us, I've thought of that as well. That's why I'm here today.'

He looks at me quizzically, even though he's used to my strange outpourings by now.

'We'll use your computer!' I add with a mischievous smile.

He doesn't understand; he tilts his head from side to side and strikes his hands against the worn arm of his chair. I've known Marino for about forty years, half his life. And yet in all that time I've never seen him change so much as the seat cover of his beloved armchair.

In the end, he stammers, 'You're mad! You know that with a computer it's the easiest thing in the world to trace the perpetrator? They'd catch us the next day.'

I think for a moment. He seems so certain that I'm almost convinced.

'And how do you know that, when you don't even know how to turn on a computer?'

'Orazio explained it to me.'

So it must be true. We'll have to go back to the original plan: handwrite a letter and slip it through the letter box. The idea came to me last night, while I was tossing and turning in bed as usual. I was thinking that the bastard who's hitting his wife should be aware that someone knows, so that the next time he'll think twice before raising a hand.

I've glimpsed the girl again, in the supermarket below our flats. I was wandering among the shelves; she was at the sausage counter. When she noticed me, she suddenly turned round so that her back was towards me, like last time. I think she's ashamed – perhaps she's worked out that I've worked it out.

At any rate I couldn't miss the opportunity. I picked up a couple of the tins of tuna on offer and walked towards her, passed behind her and whispered, 'I know.' Then I continued on my way as if nothing was wrong, without turning to check whether she'd heard me or not.

I like acting mysterious.

'But I wouldn't even know how to print a letter with that thing there. Are you absolutely sure about what you're saying? You can't accuse a man of abuse without proof. We'd ruin his life!'

There's another aspect to Marino's character that I haven't mentioned: he's good – too good. Sometimes I feel as if I'm talking to Federico, my grandson. Perhaps it's true that life goes in a circle and at the end it comes back to its starting point; in an eighty-year-old man and a baby, if you look carefully enough, you risk spotting the same fears.

'We don't need to report him. We just put a bit of pressure on him. If it isn't true that he's hitting his wife, and I've only suggested as much, he will laugh about it and move on. If, on the other hand, he is guilty as I believe, he will start looking round.'

'Cesare, you like playing the detective. Certain situations amuse you but they don't amuse me. I want to be left in peace – rash moves aren't my thing.'

It's true: I enjoy playing at being an investigator. Not just that. I love turning myself into other people, assuming different identities, living in a fantastical way. It's because up to a certain age I lived a relatively 'normal' life, without any particularly strong emotions. The problem is that as you approach the end, a lot of irritating little voices pay you a visit in the night, and whisper insistently: *Shift yourself. Don't rot at home. Do something crazy. Try and make up for everything 'not done' in your wretched life.*

There it is: the things not done. It's taken me over seventy years to work out that *I'm* there, amidst the things not done. My true essence, my desires, my energy and instinct are stored in everything I would have liked to do. It isn't nice to hear people telling you over and over again that you've been wrong all your life, that you've played your cards wrong and withdrawn from the table when you should have stayed to keep an eye on the game even if you risked losing all the chips you had in front of you. And it's never easy to recover lost time – in a few years you have to bring a life to an end. It's almost impossible. Strange how, just as you begin to understand how things work, the gong sounds, as if you were in a TV game show and started going for it in the last thirty seconds, after spending the previous three minutes staring at your fingernails.

'Marino, you're eighty now, and as far as I know you've never made a rash move in your life. You've been sitting in that armchair for ten years and if you get up your outline is still imprinted on it. Don't you think that before you die you might like to do something crazy?'

He stares straight at me and drums his fingers on the arm of his chair. I hold his gaze, so much so that I know he will be the first to give in. And sure enough, after a while, he lowers his head and whispers, 'Fine. But I warn you: if I get caught it was your idea!'

Classic Marino, doing things by halves. He probably left things unfinished when he was having sex as well. I bet that at school he was one of those boys who settled for satisfactory. He lacked the courage not to study, but at the same time it wasn't important for him to know things; he just wanted to reach the goal as soon as possible, so that he could be left in peace. If he was a topic, Marino would be a two-page essay, the statutory minimum. I, on the other hand, even in this case, could assume two different guises: an eight-page essay or a blank page. I would accept both possibilities.

'We don't have to go into a bank with balaclavas on. We just have to write a warning letter. And we're doing it for a good cause. Don't you want to help a poor girl?'

He nods, but clearly he isn't very convinced.

'Have you really not understood what we're talking about? Have you never met her on the stairs?' I ask, startled.

He merely shakes his head.

'OK, obviously you couldn't have seen her. How long is it since you've poked your nose out of this molehill?'

'It isn't a molehill!' he replies, thrusting his chest out towards me.

He's right, it isn't a molehill, but my friend needs a good sharp slap.

'Yes, Marino, this house is a molehill. Your *life* is a molehill. You aren't dead yet – can you get that into your head? The world is still out there – an asteroid hasn't collided with the world in the last ten years. There are still streets, trees, shop windows and beautiful women.'

He should be furious. In his place I'd get up and grab the arm of the person talking to me; I would hurl insults at him; I might even smack him one, after which I'd throw him out of the house. But then I'd put my coat on and charge down the stairs. Marino doesn't do any of those things: he doesn't get angry; he doesn't hit me; he doesn't move from his armchair. He looks at me and smiles. The old twit is fond of me, as I am of him, but I won't die in here just to keep him company.

I get up and walk towards the door.

He blocks my path.

'I was thinking…perhaps we could call Orazio, see what he thinks – whether they really could trace us through the computer. He could help you write the letter.'

'Yes, fine,' I say. 'That seems like a good idea to me.'

'Then I'll call him tonight and let you know.'

I shut the door and walk upstairs. I don't use the lift; I have to keep in training if I'm going to go on being an idiot.

At the first step my phone rings.

'Dad?'

'Hi, Dante,' I reply wearily.

Either I speak or I confront the stairs. I decide to stop a few steps away from my destination.

'How are you?'

'Fine.'

'OK, the other day I forgot to tell you that on Saturday evening there's the opening of an important exhibition. What are you up to? Will you come?'

'Will there be food?'

'Yes, there will be food, or else I wouldn't have called you,' he says, and sighs slowly.

'Fine. Who's the artist?'

'Leo Perotti, an emerging painter who has already shown in Berlin. I'd like to introduce you to him.'

Never heard of him in my life – I admit I'm not a great art expert. If they were showing not Perotti but Picasso I would receive the news with the same frame of mind. Dante, on the other hand, seems euphoric; his voice is slightly too high, almost strident, like a premenstrual woman.

'Fine, I'll be there,' I tell him.

I'd like to be more enthusiastic, but I can't do it. Every time I propose behaving in a different way towards Dante, when I see him or speak to him on the phone I don't move an inch. Being grumpy with my children is the only tool still at my disposal; changing my approach would require a considerable waste of energy. And I need my energy for other things.

'Is Sveva coming too?' I add.

'I don't know,' he snorts. 'I told her to drop in if she can.'

I say nothing. I have nothing to say.

Luckily he takes the next step.

'I can't wait to see you on Saturday. I'm really excited!'

I can't imagine what he could be excited about, not even if it were his exhibition. My son has an art gallery in the middle of the old town – a nice, fashionable venue, with a rather strange clientele, if I'm being honest. But I like his work, even though I'd never dream of telling him. I know it's wrong, but that's just how I am: I can't say what needs to be said. Sometimes I've tried, but the words stay on the tip of my tongue before trickling back down my gullet.

'I'm happy for you,' I say without much conviction.

He seems to notice, because he says nothing for a moment, then says goodbye and hangs up.

I'm proud of Dante – of his personality, his job and the way he goes about things. In some respects I now think he's better than his sister, and yet I still have more confidence in her. It's easier to interact with a woman, even if my daughter has her foibles. When they were little, Caterina told me off for my open preference towards Sveva, because she, to balance out the affection, was closer to our second-born son. In fact, I didn't choose. Dante arrived just as Sveva was becoming a little girl and starting to relate to me, talking, playing, hugging me. Dante struck me as resembling one of those dolls that look at you inertly from shop windows. So, without meaning to, Caterina and I shared out our children and our tasks. She looked after Dante; I looked after Sveva. He became homosexual; she egocentric and neurotic.

'If you were here, we could swap roles now. Perhaps that way we could compensate a little bit for the damage done!' I exclaim.

My words echo down the empty corridor.

'Although I think it's a bit late now. We should have thought of it before. It's your fault – you didn't want to change, you never had doubts and you thought that life had one track to follow. I must admit, even then I tended to kick out. If you'd listened to me, perhaps things might have turned out differently.'

The walls don't reply. It's better that way – at least they can't disagree. Meanwhile, the clock in the kitchen goes on ticking away the seconds. I had never realized before, but silence is the master of this house.

Chapter Nine

No One Can Be Saved If They Don't Want to Be

One of Signora Vitagliano's cats pays me a visit from time to time. The bloody mog goes out on to the balcony, circumnavigates the building and slips into my flat. I think it's partly Emma's fault, because she always leaves her window closed, so that the beast is forced to travel another few feet to find a pious soul who accepts its desire to escape Eleonora's morbid affection. And if, as now, the shutters are closed, it stays outside scratching until I'm obliged to open up.

A bit of a problem, in short, but also company. I get up and pick it up by the neck to bring it to the bed. It's half past three in the morning and getting any shut-eye is out of the question. The cat is called Fluffy, but I've nicknamed it Beelzebub. Fluffy is an appalling name; only a woman could have come up with it.

No one in the block can bear Eleonora Vitagliano because her stray cats follow her inside the building. The truth is that those cats would hurl themselves from the fifth floor for her. And what's more, she stuffs them full of food from dawn till dusk! I'd be surprised if some of them didn't suffer from cholesterol or diabetes.

And yet, at the end of the day, I like the cat lady; even as a girl she was pleasant and sunny by nature. Today she's tetchier, less open to her fellow human beings, but she doesn't cause much trouble, and she's kind to animals. And if I had reached the age I am without realizing how much animals deserve our respect, it would mean I hadn't acquired the slightest understanding of the way things are.

In any case, I've called the puss Beelzebub because it's completely black and its eyes have dazzling red reflections. A devil, in fact, which wanders around the building in search of some stupid human to offer it a nice bowl of biscuits. I don't have any to give, but the creature's incessant miaowing in the silence of the night gets on my nerves. I go into the kitchen, and freeze at the desolate spectacle of the fridge, which contains only three eggs, a bit of cooked ham, a pack of processed cheese slices, a bottle of wine and some milk. The choice boils down to ham or milk.

I sit down at the kitchen table and throw the ham to my friend, who devours it in an instant and then stays there looking at me with pleading eyes.

'I'm sorry, old pal, I have nothing else to give you. You'll have to make do with that.'

I pour him a drop of milk and me a drop of wine, and begin to reflect on this fairly ridiculous scene: I'm sitting in the dead of night in the company of an animal, each of us with his nose in a drink. Luckily mine is a lot stronger.

But I wouldn't mind being a cat, one that isn't really tied to anyone, one that 'decides' to love because basically it doesn't need to and can get by perfectly well on its own. I like people who get by without annoying anyone else. There, if I had to be reborn as an animal (which, given my many sins, is a possibility that should not be discounted), I would like to be a cat. I would find a cat lady to sponge off, and I'd go off all day looking for some little puss-cat to woo. I'd be one of those dirty cats with a big head and dark eyes who wander among the rubbish bins like cheetahs among the trees of the savannah. Marino, on the other hand, would be a Persian or a Siamese, one of those breeds which have adapted to domesticity over the centuries, becoming incapable of living in the streets. It has taken generations for a Persian to turn into a sybarite in need of others, while it's only taken Marino a single lifetime.

A dull thud comes from the landing.

Beelzebub turns round just for a moment, and immediately comes back to his milk.

I get up and step into the corridor.

'Open up, you whore!'

I look through the spyhole and see him, the wife beater, thumping his front door and ranting. 'You lousy bitch, open up right now, or you'll be sorry!'

He seems drunk. I've got to do something, but if I think about it too hard I won't do anything.

I open the door.

He turns round and looks at me as if he'd just seen a Martian coming out of a flying saucer.

'So? What way is that to speak to a young lady?'

I don't know what the hell I'm doing. I'm acting out of instinct. Sometimes you either act instinctively or you don't do anything at all.

'What the hell do you want?'

He reeks of alcohol and he seems pretty drunk to me. Perhaps I should shut the door and get back to my drink, but I'm too proud. And then, damn it, who would be brave enough to punch a poor old man?

'You've woken me up and you're also upsetting your wife – that's what I want to sort out!'

He comes over and stares right into my eyes. Then, with

stinking breath, he puts his thoughts into words. 'Go fuck yourself!' he snaps.

Marino, in my place, would lower his eyes, apologize and retreat into his flat. But I'm me, and Cesare Annunziata is not like other old men. If someone steps on my toes I'll react, even if it means getting my leg broken. So I stage one of my classic little scenes, those scenes that I'm really good at.

'You jerk, you're talking to a retired army general. Kindly moderate your tone or I will wipe that idiotic expression off your face!'

He steps back and I grin with satisfaction. The army general works every time.

The bastard is about to say something in reply, but at that moment the door opens and she appears in the doorway. The man packages all his accumulated rage into the expression that he turns on his wife, then he hurls himself into the house and disappears.

Emma, on the other hand, stays in the doorway and turns towards me.

I smile, proud of myself, but the lady doesn't seem very happy.

'And what do you want of *me*? Mind your own business. No one's asked you to do anything!' And she closes the door.

I stay on the landing, still with that half-smile stamped across my face, then I snort irritably and go to the bathroom. I have to pee, as always happens when I get angry or agitated. I sit down on the toilet and in comes Beelzebub to rub himself against my wrinkled calves. I turn to him, the only creature I have to talk to.

'And there was I almost getting myself killed to defend her! I'm a stupid, romantic, old fool. No one can be saved if they don't want to be. I haven't worked that out in almost eighty years!'

Beelzebub looks at me with some alarm, then decides not to waste his time with a foolish old man who talks to himself, and stops to lick his paw. I've always found it a brilliant way of washing: economical, it doesn't pollute the atmosphere and it doesn't make you waste time. Except that we should have been made double-jointed with prehensile tongues. I often wonder why we were made so complex, what need there was for all those organs, capillaries, blood, intestines, nails, hair? Couldn't we come up with a simpler alternative? And why do we need energy from outside, from food and water? Or oxygen? Why can't we be self-sufficient? It's a complex subject and if I sit here for much longer I won't be able to feel my legs and I'll have to call the emergency services to get back to bed.

The bell rings. Beelzebub runs for shelter under the sofa. I look at the time: it's a quarter past four. Tonight's busier than usual. It might be Emma wanting to apologize, or maybe her husband who's had another think and wants to punch me. I stop half-way down the corridor and prick up my ears. The bell rings again, briefly. My tormentor wants to kill me but, at the same time, he's worried about waking up the whole building. For a fraction of a second, I'm tempted to go back to bed and use the earplugs that I still keep in the bedside-table drawer, then I think about Marino's moony face and open the door. If I'm going to die I'd rather do it while I'm still alive.

In front of me is the frail outline of Eleonora Vitagliano, in dressing gown and slippers.

'Hello,' I begin.

'Hello. Forgive the time, but I need to talk to you.'

I'm not used to letting women into my flat, particularly

when I'm in my pyjamas, but the word 'woman' isn't appropriate for my neighbour.

As soon as I open the door, Beelzebub comes running.

'Darling, this is where you've got to!' she says, and picks up the thuggish cat which has already forgotten yours truly and the ham it cadged off me.

'Cesare, I saw what happened a moment ago...' She imagines she whispers, but because she's deaf the volume of her voice is entirely out of kilter with her facial expression.

'Ah,' I observe, not knowing what else to say.

'You did right to step in,' she goes on. 'That character needs someone to stand up to him.'

I nod and stay in the doorway, waiting for the old thing to understand and leave me alone. Instead she stays there, with Fluffy in her arms, staring me intently in the face.

'Eleonora, it's four in the morning...' I try to say, but she isn't even listening.

'I think that man hits his wife!'

I open my eyes wide. So the old dear is less senile than I thought.

'What do you know about it?'

'What?'

I turn my voice up a notch. 'I said...Are you sure?'

'Yes, yes, I'm sure. You know, I don't hear very well, but those two have been making such a racket recently...'

'Yes...'

'Only the other night I saw them coming home and she had a cloth over her mouth.'

'Anyway, the girl told me not to get involved, so I'm not going to,' I answer brusquely.

'And what if something happens?'

'It won't be my fault.'

'We could call the police.'

'You call them! I was about to be attacked, and I got an earful too. However, Eleonora, I understand your concern, I really do, but you know what it's like. It's late…'

'Yes, forgive me. You're right. The fact is that I can't get to sleep at night these days.'

'Yes, I understand.'

Life is strange. When you are young and strong you always get to sleep; when you become spineless and idling about seems a good way of passing the time, shutting your eyes is out of the question.

'But if those two argue again I'll call you,' she says as she steps back on to the landing.

'Fine,' I reply.

I'd be capable of promising her anything at all at that moment.

I say goodbye to her and that two-faced cat and shut the door behind them.

I glance at the clock again: it's half past four in the morning. There's no point trying to get to sleep now – it makes more sense to put the coffee on to boil.

What a great night! A drink with an admiring cat, an argument in the course of which I nearly got myself killed, a scolding from a disagreeable neighbour who I was trying to defend and a chat with Eleonora Vitagliano. It's a good thing the sun will be up shortly. In the meantime, I think I should have a shower. The people in the building are right: the cat lady might well be nice, but, God, she stinks.

Chapter Ten

The First of Three Unattainable Women

When you reach my age, inevitably you start drawing up a balance of your own life: the things you've done and the things you've lost, the bad deals you've made, the opportunities you've missed. But since I've never liked drawing up balances I've avoiding doing it and still do. Whatever you want to say, if I were to land on the planet another ten times, I'd still travel the same journey and crash into the same rocks along the way. Most of us are like ants: we follow a trail that has already been laid for us. So, don't worry, I'm not going to bore you with a list of complaints; instead I will talk about women, who remain, in my opinion, one of the chief reasons for living.

I've had lots: pretty, ugly, nice and nasty, kind and mean. And I have never loved any of them as much as the only three I couldn't have. You know, a thing you've enjoyed, whether it's a car, a house, a job, even a woman, is consumed like wax in a flame. But you do get used to what you don't have. So, even now that I'm an old buffer whose sole hope lies in the altruism (so to speak) of Rossana, the only ladies who come in search of me in the silence of the night, apart from my wife, are those three harpies who refused to lie by my side.

Anna was a schoolmate of mine. Fair hair, green eyes, big bazumbas. I fell in love as soon as I saw her. Even then, in fact, I had an unfashionable enthusiasm for curvaceous figures. The problem was that she was older than me, albeit by only a year. And yet for children those three hundred and sixty-five extra days make all the difference; in the period of time it takes the earth to rotate around the sun, a woman has already understood that you, a small and insignificant creature from the class below, are worth about as much as the gum stuck under her desk.

A moment comes in everyone's life when we work out that the romantic stories of impossible love affairs that grand-parents and old aunts told us are simply nonsense. Love is much cruder than an old relative serving up the 'truth' to you, which means that you can have a lovely smile, write love poems to your princess or serenade her below her balcony, but if your face is a sea of pimples and your breath stinks she's going to go out with someone else. So you have to wait for your last year of school to launch your assault. And, thinking about it, that's how it was. The time spent secretly tailing her (or, in the toilet, devoting to her brief and fleeting moments of passion) taught me that if you really desire something, then waiting turns into hope and makes time worth living.

I was as head over heels in love with Anna as only a young pup who knows nothing of life's snares could be. And that is, in fact, the right age to lose your head over a girl: if you don't learn to love at fifteen, you never will. When I approached her that day, I had already desired her for three years, I knew where she lived, who her best friends were, even her exes. But she knew nothing about me.

I don't think I'm mistaken when I say that what I later became was due to that fateful moment. A simple act changed the rest of my life. Because by the time I came home I was convinced that I was engaged. I even told my mother, who smiled and went back to the stove. At the time I placed no importance on her shrug, when I should really have asked the reason for her scepticism. The next day I went over to Anna and hugged her. She looked at me in alarm, pulled away and asked me what I was doing. A kiss was just a kiss; we certainly wouldn't have had to get married to have one of those. The problem was that for me it was the first time. First times should be exclusively for neophytes, otherwise the party who has already been through the experience extinguishes, without meaning to, the wonder in the other. Anna ruined my first kiss. Then I thought that in order to conquer her I would really have to do something much more difficult: share the 'first time' with her. In short, I had to take her to bed.

It took me eleven months to put the plan into action, months in which I assumed the role of the friend who could be trusted, the friend who accompanied her wherever she went, the friend who gave her advice, who was always there if he was needed, a bit like a little lapdog. In every respect I was perfect. Except that you don't get engaged to a friend and, in fact, she went around with other boys, certainly not with me. But then her father died, and I admit that it was a great coup for me, because Anna needed me even more. In the end, one day, we were amusing ourselves more than usual on my bed, talking about her father. If it had been up to me, I would have spent the rest of the evening listening to the thousand anecdotes about her father, which didn't interest me at all, but at some point she hugged me and turned to face me. She was still talking, except that her mouth was very close to mine; even if I'd wanted to I couldn't have pursued the conversation as if nothing was happening. So we kissed again and, in a few moments, we found ourselves half naked under the covers.

I still remember the sensation; my skin can relive the moment to infinity. It's true that the things we guard passionately never die, a bit like my grandparents' house, which I can still revisit even now if I close my eyes.

The fact remains that I was there. A few moments longer and I would have given her a 'first time' too; I would have become for ever one of the things that she would guard with jealousy. But, as we know, love doesn't deceive us – if anything, it prefers to strike us right in the face with a well-aimed slap. At the crucial moment she stopped me, took my face in her hands and said, 'Cesare, I'm sorry. I'm fond of you, but I'm only going to do that with the man of my life!'

I would be really curious to know if she kept her promise. I would like to meet her and ask her: 'You see? Your noble principle was a load of nonsense! Couldn't you have made an exception that evening? And who says I couldn't have been the man of your life?'

Instead I said nothing, I got dressed, I kissed her chastely on the cheek and walked her home. We never saw each other again, she got engaged a short time later and I went off on military service. After a few years I discovered that she had moved north with her husband. I never met her again; as far as I know she might even be dead.

Anna was my first experience of *unrequited love* – a pointless invention, thinking about it. There are so many lonely people in the world who could meet, love, be happy, have children, betray and then leave each other, while instead many waste time pursuing someone who is barely aware of their existence.

And yet this story has taught me one lesson: people who are bad-tempered, sulky and suspicious aren't really bad; it's just that, unlike everyone else, they haven't been able to work out the truth, that the world is no place for the good.

I was good. Then along came Anna, with her kick up the arse.

I should tell the story to my children, explain to Sveva that I too was a better man before life taught me to look around warily, like a hare leaving its form to look for food. The animal has a sense of danger in its DNA – it is born ready to defend itself from predators – while I wasted my first twenty years learning how to protect myself against my fellows.

Life on Earth should be like a journey to the East, an experience that opens the mind and turns us into special beings. Instead the precise opposite happens: they drag us out of the black hole when we are snow-white and put us in a box after we have tried on all the colours. I think that something, in the scrap of time that we have down here, isn't working as it should.

Chapter Eleven

Emma

Like all old people, I have my little obsessions; nothing particularly mad, excuse me, just a few rules to follow to feel a bit more at my ease. For example, I wipe the toilet seat with lavatory paper before sitting down. No harm if it's a public toilet – the problem is that I use the same technique in my house. I'm protecting myself against my own germs. It's a habit that goes back to my youth, when I worked at Partenope Services, an agency on Via dei Tribunali, in the middle of the old town. A lowly job, I admit, but at the time I was a boy full of hope, who believed in the fairy tale that life is a ladder to be approached step by step and which, in the end, will bring you to Paradise. That everything had to be conquered a bit at a time, and with major sacrifices along the way. But the years have taught me that the climb is not so simple, because often the stairs are wet and the rungs yield under your weight.

In the end, I worked out that the tale of the initial sacrifice for which, one far-off day, I will be repaid, is an idiocy invented by adults to harness the enthusiasm of the very young. There is no one up there to measure your commitment and pay you back for the energies you have expended. In fact, the years when everyone invites you to grit your teeth to build a future for yourself are the best, and shouldn't be thrown away on thinking of the years to come – which are not, in any case, worth a fraction of the ones you've had already.

Partenope Services had three employees apart from myself, two men in their late fifties and a secretary my age. It isn't hard to imagine who was to blame for the lavatory seat always being splashed. I put up with it for a while, and then one afternoon the secretary revealed the trick to me, and since then I have never been able to rest my buttocks on cold plastic. After a few months, however, I jacked it in. I took away three things from that experience: an obsession with covering the lavatory seat; the awareness that I wasn't planning on throwing away the best years of my life to take care of the worst; and Luisa, the secretary who gave me the momentous advice. Of the three, only the first two accompanied me throughout my whole life. I lost Luisa at the first bend.

In any case, as I said, the obsessions which fill a doddering old man's day are few in number. Apart from lavatory paper, for example, there is the absolute inability to accept knots. Put like that, it sounds as crazy as anything; in reality, not so much. The truth is that I find them disagreeable; I hate having to untie them. And I'm not talking about the knots of life – I mean more material things. The telephone line that twists itself into a tangle, so that lifting the receiver is impossible. But also the knots in plastic bags, or the wires behind the television, which tangle themselves up all by themselves. Or shoelaces, when they refuse to untie. That's why, over the years, I've organized myself and only wear moccasins and use cordless phones. I tell other people that it's because of my fingers, which no longer have the strength to perform small and repetitive gestures, but in fact I just get annoyed; I haven't the patience or the time to waste to untie wires and strings that will only become entangled again anyway.

And then there's Naples, the most consistent knot of all. The problem is that I've chosen the worst city to be born in. Here you can't enjoy relations with your neighbour; here everyone wants to know your business. So I've developed survival techniques to control my sociopathic urges. If I notice someone who lives in the flats waiting for the lift, I stop and open the postbox and examine it until the invader of my privacy decides to go upstairs without waiting for me. Or else I avoid standing in queues. Neapolitans can't stand and wait nicely and quietly; they feel obliged to home in on their neighbours, to chat about this and that while they wait their turn. Whether it's at the post office or the bank, the supermarket or the cinema, queues in Naples are a medium for chattering and getting free information about other people's lives. Even the barber's below my house is a natural meeting place for citizens in need of gossip. So when it's time to have my hair cut I call a taxi and have myself taken to another part of town.

Shopping, on the other hand, is much more complicated. Beside the entrance to my building there's a deli, a butcher's and a greengrocer's – a firing squad looking you up and down to guess, even if it's only from your movements, some new indiscretion that might bring a little interest into their empty lives. For years I haven't crossed the threshold of their shops and, in fact, I even avoid walking in front of them; I cross the road, walk a short distance on the opposite pavement and come back on the other side. All three will have noticed, but I don't care. The important thing is to escape their trap. I've nicknamed them 'the good, the bad and the ugly'. The ugly one is the greengrocer: old, dirty and scruffy, with just three teeth in his mouth and fingernails that are always black; he only ever speaks in strong local dialect and you can't make out a word that he says. Many times in the past I found myself staring into the void after his observations about apricots or peaches. The good one is the deli owner: a nice person, always smiling, who distracts himself among the tins, the sliced meats and the pointless chatter of all his customers. The bad one, last of all, is the butcher. In fact, he's a regular chap; he's nice too. The problem is his wife. She's the one who controls the conversation; she's the one who fires questions at you while you're waiting for your pork loin. She's a harbinger of chatter, the local gang leader from which all the others take their lead.

The issue is that things don't go much better at the supermarket. Until I actually find myself wandering around the shelves, I can still hope that I'm going to manage; I just have to ignore the pensioner who's trying to buttonhole me by talking about the rudeness of an assistant or the girl who bumped him with her trolley. But the problem arises at the sausage counter. There's always a lady there who, while she's waiting, talks to the employee on duty and, usually, with the lady beside her as well. A gang of three which, depending on the slowness of the shop assistant, can grow out of all proportion until it encompasses several others within earshot. Luckily, after careful study, I have managed to work out which of the assistants is the fastest, and if he isn't there I carry straight on. Once I've reached the tills, I aim for the quickest one, manna for phobics like me, and slip furtively outside. Once I'm close to home, I walk back and forth for a while before finally putting the key in the lock of the front door. Only then can I say that I'm almost safe. At any rate I never turn back; I know already that the good, the bad and the ugly have their eyes fixed on my shoulders, weary from the weight of my obsessions.

When I close the door to the building, I am welcomed by a miaow. Perched on the stairs is Beelzebub, who looks at me seraphically as he tries to decipher the contents of the bag that I'm carrying. The cat has superior intelligence – every time I go to the supermarket he waits for me in the hall to miaow charmingly and rub sycophantically as soon as he notices the shopping bag.

There are a few envelopes in the postbox. I leave them there and reach the lift. Thirty years ago I stopped believing that anything good could come out of a postbox. As we know, good news doesn't come to find you at home. I don't understand how my former colleagues can still maintain their unshakeable faith in a stroke of luck. They spend their pensions on scratch cards or the lottery in the hope of changing their lives. And yet they should have worked out that if the goddess of fortune didn't kiss them when they were attractive and in good shape, she certainly isn't about to now that they have hairs coming out of their noses, no teeth in their mouth and cataracts in their eyes. Amongst other things, after a certain age what are you going to do with a win of millions? You just risk your children falling out over your legacy.

I open the lift door.

'Come on then, lovely,' I say, turning to Beelzebub, who stares at me for a moment and then weaves quickly between my legs.

I press the button and glance admiringly at the puss, a rebellious animal that refuses to moulder away in Signora Vitagliano's house, but wants to explore, to snatch something from everybody and exploit his neighbour. He's a villainous cat, is Beelzebub, and I like villains. In this block, in any case, he has found his harem – there are lots of flats that he can slip into, some of them filled with food, others only with memories. The flats aren't all the same – some of them open and close several times a day, while others remain closed all the time. Some smell of clean laundry and tomato juice, others of cardboard and damp. And the second of these, generally speaking, are more trustworthy – they've stayed standing in spite of everything, waiting for someone to come back and take care of them.

Reaching my floor, I set down the bag of shopping and take my keys from my coat. At that moment, the neighbours' door opens and Emma appears again, the woman I fought for in vain. We look at one another briefly, then I try to turn the keys in the lock, not an easy manoeuvre if your hands are trembling like a trampoline after someone's just jumped on it.

'Here, let me help you,' she says.

I let her come outside, even though my self-esteem takes a knock as unexpected as it is ill-timed. But I don't want to have anything to do with this woman – the sooner I get rid of her, the better. She concludes the operation and smiles at me. I think she's trying to apologize.

'Thanks!' I say brightly and pick up my bag.

Beelzebub runs into the flat.

I wait in the doorway for my neighbour to decide on her next move. She stares at me steadily so that I notice she has a swollen cheekbone. There's something in her that attracts me, apart from her beauty. Perhaps because she reminds me a bit of Sveva when she was a teenager, even if this one's teenage years are long ago.

I don't know what to do. Emma doesn't move. Perhaps she wants to come in, perhaps she wants to talk, and yet she doesn't do either. She stands there as if frozen, staring at me. Then I take charge of the tempation situation. I may be a poor old man who can't get a key in a lock, but I'm still not comfortable in the role of being an idiot when there's a woman present.

'Do you want to come in?' I ask.

She nods.

'Be my guest,' I say, and accompany the word with a movement of my arm.

Emma immerses herself gently, quietly in my world, rather as Beelzebub did that first time. She's trying to work out if it's friendly territory, or if there's some danger hidden in the corner of the kitchen.

'Can I get you something?' I ask.

She nods again, as if she's lost her tongue.

I slip off my coat and walk to the stove. The girl follows me and sits down at the kitchen table, piled up with underpants and socks. If you live alone for too long, you start thinking that your intimacy is inviolable. I apologize and pick up the garments to take them to the bedroom, but a rebellious sock slips from the group and hurls itself to the floor, so that when I come back it's still there, at the feet of my unexpected guest.

'I wanted to say sorry for my behaviour the other evening,' she begins.

'Don't worry,' I answer straight away. 'Water under the bridge.'

In fact, I haven't forgotten the snub, but rancour is a major shortcoming of old people, and I don't want to be like an old person.

I open the fridge. I have nothing to offer her but the usual bottle of red wine that keeps me company in the evening. I pick it up by the neck and put it on the table along with two glasses. Then I sit down facing her. I don't understand what this wonderful girl wants of me, and I'm not used to having guests these days. Apart from Beelzebub, obviously.

'My husband is going to kill me sooner or later,' Emma says at last, looking me so straight in the eyes that I find it hard to hold her gaze. Her toneless, lifeless voice contrasts with her youthful appearance, which she maintains in spite of everything.

I fill the glasses without even asking her permission and she doesn't stop me.

Beelzebub appears in the kitchen, his stomach already protesting.

'Have you told anyone? Your parents, a friend?'

'No, I've got no one here, and anyway I would never admit it. People judge.'

I sip the red liquid and study the young woman. If I were half the age I am, I would resolve the situation in my own way, but instead I find myself choking back my rage. For some reason she thinks that I don't judge. Perhaps she doesn't care about the opinion of an old neighbour who stands to share the information with the building's cat at most.

'How long has this been going on?'

She lowers her head and starts tapping her fingers on her glass, then she whispers, 'Three years.'

I look at her, startled.

'The first time it was because I dropped a painting. He hit me on the neck with a wooden spoon. I can still hear the dull thud in my ears. I went out wearing a scarf for a month.'

I put my glass in the sink and pick up my cigarettes from the shelf, the first thing that comes to mind when I feel anxious.

'No, please…' she says.

I freeze and give her a look half-way between curiosity and annoyance.

'I'm pregnant.'

I close my eyes and slump on the arm of the chair. Why can't I mind my own business? This is too much even for a Methuselah like me.

'How many weeks?'

'Two months.'

'Does he know?'

'No.'

'Do you want to have an abortion?'

'No.'

I sit there in silence. Perhaps she's come to ask me for some financial help, perhaps just a bit of understanding and affection. Perhaps she needs a father. *Sorry, my dear, I struggle to play that part even with my own children.*

'You should tell him.'

'I'd like to leave, but I don't know how. He would come looking for me.'

'Why are you telling me?'

'Because you wanted to see. Most people, even if they have their suspicions, give you a compassionate look and turn the other way. People still think these are private matters that need to be resolved in the family.'

'Have you approached any kind of charity?'

'No, I'd be ashamed.'

With me, though, she isn't ashamed. And yet I'm not the kind of person that people like to open up to. Sveva, for example, never has done, and even Dante hides his sexual tastes from me. This stranger has confided more to me in ten minutes than my children have in their whole lives.

'Where is he now?'

'Out of town. He comes back tomorrow.'

Silence falls between us again, and the ticking of the clock on the wall occupies the space for a few seconds, before a miaow from Beelzebub reminds me that the poor creature is still waiting to be fed. Now I decide to offer my neighbour the only thing in my possession: a bit of bonhomie.

'OK, the cat is starving and I'm beginning to flag myself.

Why don't we stop here? I propose some spaghetti with fresh tomato sauce.'

'I'd love some,' she says.

I get to my feet, pick up the pan, fill it with water and put it on the flame. Then I take the tomatoes from the shopping bag, which is still on the table, and start chopping them.

She gets up as well and comes and stands beside me. 'Let me do it. You lay the table.'

I look at her in confusion before passing her the knife. For five years no woman has used my kitchen; for five years I've had supper without laying the table. I start rummaging among the drawers in search of an old tablecloth, while Emma starts talking again, as if she can't help it. If you lift a weight off your shoulders you have to go the whole way. A bit like when you go for a pee, you can't stop half-way and get back to your business.

'I underestimated the signs. I didn't pay attention to the alarm bells. At first he didn't hit me, but he flew off the handle over nothing. I told myself he was just very stressed, that it would pass, that basically nothing had happened. So I decided to put up with it. I tried to convince myself that with my support he would calm down.'

I can't find the tablecloth. And yet I'm sure there was one. I miss Caterina more than ever.

'One evening I managed to escape and took refuge in a bar. But when it closed he came and brought me home. And he gave me a kicking and broke a rib. Then there were more blows and rows. In the end I was almost convinced that it was my fault, that I was making his life impossible.'

I'm struggling for breath, and not because I'm bending down under the furniture in the kitchen in search of some phantom tablecloth, but because I can't go on listening to this terrible story. It's as if someone were clinging to my back and demanding to be carried. I've never done that, even with Sveva. Once I tried to do it with Federico, but as soon as he was on my shoulders he felt a *crack* along my spine and had to stop. After that I vowed never to play with my grandson again. Sorry, but playing reminds me that I'm old and, as I've said, I don't like to be fooled on the subject.

'You should report him,' is all I manage to say.

'No, he'd kill me before the trial started. And even if I left, he'd come after me.'

I give up: there isn't a single tablecloth. I must have given them to Sveva as a souvenir of her mother.

'So what do you plan to do?'

She turns and stares at me. In the meantime, she stirs the tomato sauce with the wooden spoon.

'I don't know. I just want a bit of peace.'

Peace is very overrated. We think it's a natural state from which we part company every now and again, when in fact it's precisely the opposite. In life, peace comes and pays us a visit only very rarely, and often we aren't even aware of it.

'I haven't got a tablecloth…' I admit.

She looks at me and smiles, then brings her hand to her painful cheekbone and becomes serious again. 'It doesn't matter. We'll eat without it,' she says.

That hint of a smile enrages me, and for a moment I really consider opening the door, going to my neighbour's flat and beating him up, whatever the cost. Then I remember that he isn't there.

'Have you been seen by a doctor?' I ask.

'No, but I think my cheekbone's broken. I put ice on it from time to time.'

I walk over to her and, without a word, rest my finger on the bruised bone. The skin is purple and swollen with fluid. Emma doesn't flinch.

'If you don't report him, I will!' I say at last.

'No, please don't. I'm scared. And I'll be homeless and jobless. He doesn't want me to work.'

I sigh. Another woman coming to me with a problem, who won't accept a solution. Except that this time I can't look the other way and pretend nothing's wrong.

'It's ready,' she says at last.

I pass her the plates. Emma fills them with swift, sure movements.

We sit down at the table. The spaghetti is really good, much better than I had anticipated.

'For some reason mine is never as good as this,' I admit.

She smiles, ignoring the pain this time. *Good for you, Emma, smiling even when it hurts.*

The cat starts wailing. I'd forgotten him. I get up and take a slice of cheese and a bit of ham from the fridge. Beelzebub is monomaniacal on the subject – if it was up to him we'd only eat meat. I'd be really curious to know his triglyceride levels, although I very much doubt that they're higher than mine. I stopped analysing blood when I worked out that by checking my levels I was deluding myself that I could control my life. I would have been wasting my time if, at my age, I hadn't realized that nothing can be controlled and the only thing we're given to do is live.

'Is that your cat?'

'Heavens, no. It belongs to Signora Vitagliano, our neighbour. The poor mog manages to escape her clutches every now and again.'

Emma smiles again, then the sound of forks on plates dominates the scene for a few minutes.

'Do you live alone?' she asks eventually.

'Yes, I do. My wife died five years ago.'

'I'm sorry,' she whispers and dives back into her food.

With her head lowered and her long dark hair falling to her knees, she looks more than ever like Sveva. Incredible, but I've only just realized that my daughter has never come for supper at my house. It's hard for her to come here – too many memories of her mother. I think the fact that I'm still alive is a mere detail.

'I have a daughter older than you who looks very like you,' I say.

'Is she married?'

'Yes,' I say, and for a moment I'm tempted to talk to her about the humdrum nature of my daughter's life.

'And then there's Dante, who you've met.'

'Is he married too?'

'No, he's gay,' I say, before bringing the glass to my lips. It was a pointless clarification, but it's stronger than me – every time I talk about him I find myself spontaneously slipping out with something.

'I could tell,' is all she says.

'Why don't you go to your parents' house?' I ask once I've cleared my plate.

'I ran away from home at fourteen. My dad drank and picked fights with me and Mum. That's why I left as soon as I could. Just think, I swore to myself that I would never be bound to a man...'

Some lives run along pre-established tracks and there's never a dramatic scene that changes the direction of things. Even life sometimes manages to be banal.

'But I don't feel like talking any more today,' she adds firmly.

I nod. I like this girl. Like Rossana, she doesn't mince her words.

'Why don't we watch a bit of television?'

'Television?'

'Yeah. You must have a TV, right?'

'Of course,' I reply and get to my feet.

She's acting as if she were my granddaughter and this house her place of refuge. Grandparents' houses are often places where runaway grandchildren can seek shelter.

I don't watch much TV, and then only documentaries. Sometimes I actually have to force myself to turn it on – partly because I don't want to end up like Marino, partly because I've watched it too much in my life.

We sit down on the sofa, side by side, and I find myself smiling. Life really is strange: suddenly you find yourself sharing your table and your sitting room with people who wouldn't have acknowledged your existence the day before.

A few moments later, Beelzebub jumps on to the sofa and curls up between our bodies.

'I'm happy when he's not there,' she says as she changes channels. 'Even if the house is sometimes too quiet,' she adds a few moments later.

'I'm here if you need me,' I say.

'Thank you very much,' she replies, not even turning round.

A few moments more, and I start again.

'You want to know something?' I ask, and this time she looks at me. 'A woman I loved very much had the same name as you. Emma.'

She draws up her knees and says, 'Your wife?'

'No.'

'*Then who?*' her face seems to ask.

'It's a long story,' I add and turn back to face the television.

We sit there in silence, watching the screen, until I notice that my eyes are closing. It's bedtime really – at the end of the day I'm old, after all.

I turn round and find Emma curled up fast asleep. It makes her look even more defenceless. For some reason some people have no guardian angels. I'm a long way from being an angel, and yet it feels natural to get up and find her a blanket. I wrap Emma in warm plaid, turn off the television, then the light, and go to bed. In the silence of the flat, the only sound is the purring of Beelzebub cuddled up by the feet of this defenceless creature who has decided to wake me from my torpor.

I would like to come to your aid, to help you to save yourself, Emma. Really I would. But I fear I'm not up to it. One life wasn't enough for me to learn how to hold out a hand without trembling.

Chapter Twelve

Superman in a Skirt

In my day the guests at a party were treated with respect – they were served reverentially. Now we've got buffets, a way like any other to complicate the lives of the poor people who have already been forced to don their best clothes, take a taxi and appear at the party with forced smiles. As far as I'm concerned that's not how it actually worked: I didn't put on special clothes, just the things I put on every day. I stopped complicating my life in that way when I reached old age, given that no one is ever going to tell an old man that he's dressed inappropriately. But the people around me are rather smart. They walk around the room pretending to admire Perotti's paintings, but in fact they're much more interested in the trays of food. The problem is that it's impossible to get anywhere near the table: some of the guests have managed to make it to the front and are not about to budge. Luckily I'm old, and old people sit down to wait for their relatives to bring them a nice plate of food.

'Here you are,' says Sveva, handing me one.

That's what a daughter is for. Dante doesn't really think about food – he wanders from one painting to another, smiling, supplying explanations, shaking hands, greeting people obsequiously.

'Why is your brother so reverential with these people?' I ask provocatively.

'Reverential? I don't think so. He's just being nice.'

'There's a subtle difference.'

'Yes, and you don't know it.'

My daughter can't stand me. I've got to take control and do something. But even thinking about confronting the problem bores me.

'What about your husband?' I ask, changing the subject.

'He's working till late.'

As ever, once a marriage hits the rocks, people start working late, having meeting after meeting, being suddenly called away on business.

We sit in silence, side by side. She looks at the people; I look at her. For some reason Sveva hates me. And yet, when she was little I paid her lots of attention. Perhaps if I'd left her in the care of her mother she'd be different now. If you try to bring up a child you can only get it wrong; if you let things be, you may end up with an adult who doesn't blame you for their shortcomings.

'What's up? Are you having difficulties?'

She turns round, her eyes wide with alarm. And I don't think I've ever actually asked her such a question before. Caterina was there for that.

'Why? What makes you think so?'

'Well, there's never any sign of him and if I ask you questions you give me irritable replies.'

'When do you ask me anything? When have you ever asked me anything? What's this new thing that's happening?'

'You see? You're being aggressive. Women do that when they think they've been cornered,' I reply casually, before grabbing a glass of Prosecco offered to me by a pleasant waiter.

'What a joke, you talking about women!' she says, and takes the glass from my hand. 'Will you stop drinking? Or are you determined to kill yourself?'

I snort. 'Sveva, you're boring.'

She smiles and takes my hand. I want to pull it back, so that I don't look like a senile old man being consoled by his patient daughter, but she's gripping it too firmly.

'In fact, I'm doing just fine. But how are you getting on?'

'Very well, as ever.'

'Yes,' she answers bitterly, 'it's true.'

'What?'

'You're very good at being on your own. It's only in company that you've got a few problems.'

My daughter knows me well. Which is very useful: I don't need to explain things to her. I like women who don't ask any questions.

'I'm not drawn to people, I admit it.'

We watch the people munching canapés as they stroll from one painting to another, until eventually Sveva gets up and says, 'Why don't you go and talk to Dante for a while? You've been sitting on this chair since you got here.'

'Well, it's comfortable. And if I get up someone will take my place.'

'Do as you like. But I think he'd like a comment from you, or even just a smile.'

Then she disappears into the crowd. I'm no longer the right age for being a father: too many responsibilities. I've been unlucky: if Caterina were here now she'd go and congratulate Dante and listen to the story of Perotti's artistic career, and I could sit here drinking Prosecco and watching people. If my wife had been here, she would have gone to pick up Federico from school the other day, and I wouldn't have seen the SUV driver's hand on my daughter's thigh.

Instead my wife is dead and she's washed her hands of everything. It's just as well I was the selfish one.

I get up, take another glass of Prosecco and walk over to a painting, a kind of photograph retouched on the computer: in the background the American flag and in the foreground Superman with a big 'S' printed on his chest and...wearing a miniskirt!

'What do you think? Do you like it?'

I turn round. Beside me there's a man in his forties with a beige velvet jacket, holding a glass of red wine. He's wearing a top hat.

'Well, let's say it's amusing.'

He smiles. 'Yes, I think so too.'

I turn back towards the painting, trying to shake him off, but he soon launches off again: 'You're Dante's father, aren't you?'

Christ, there's nothing worse than a sociable person. What's so great about meeting a new individual? We're all the same anyway, more or less, a collection of shortcomings walking along the street and trying to avoid similar collections.

'Yes.'

'Dante talks about you a lot.'

'Really?'

'Yes,' he replies.

He's pleased to have captured my attention. The poor thing doesn't imagine that my attention is focused entirely on a woman behind him, with an enormous bosom like Rossana's. If I were younger, I would have to try and work out the source of that fixation and maybe read Freud, but I'm old, so I can just get on with staring at breasts without worrying too much about it. At any rate, I need to shake that fake artist off my heels. I swallow the last gulp and hand the glass to my interlocutor, who looks at me curiously.

'Will you hang on to it for me? I need to go to the toilet.'

He smiles awkwardly and takes the glass. I go to the toilet, blow my nose, look in the mirror, fart, flush and open the door. Waiting by the washbasins is the beautiful woman with the big bosom, who studies me severely. Perhaps she heard the noise. She asks if she can go in, but I try to stop her, at least until the fetid stench of my colon has faded away. The lady looks at me impatiently as I go on smiling at her like an idiot.

'So, can I get past?'

'Of course, of course,' I reply and move away.

At least she has achieved her goal. When I get back to the gallery, the man in the top hat has been swallowed up by the crowd. I take advantage of the fact to go over to Dante, who is talking to a little group of four people who are listening to him attentively. Every now and again he turns towards the painting behind him and points out a detail. He's gay – that's just how it is. I don't understand why it is that if you prefer cock you have to move and gesticulate like an imbecile. Women don't have attitudes like that. His audience must have noticed by now. Perhaps they don't care. It seems to me that it's getting worse and worse by the day.

And yet, as I said before, the role of father no longer appeals to me. Over the years I've become too sincere, with myself and others. If my son bats for the other team I'm going to mention the fact, even if I think he should behave as he sees fit. I just wish he had the courage to admit it to me. What does he think I would say? When I couldn't care less if he went to be with some crazy tart or a hairy bald man? Christ, I shudder to imagine the scene.

Dante notices me and beckons me over so that he can introduce me to his guests. I shake hands without listening to names that I would forget in a second anyway.

Once we're on our own, he comes out with the classic question: 'So, do you like it?'

I look around and say, 'Yes, it's lovely.'

'I thought the paintings might be a bit too surreal for your taste.'

'That means you don't know me very well. I like all things surreal. It's reality that bores me.'

Dante seems pleased by the reply.

'But I wanted to ask you: who's the lady in blue?'

'Which one?'

'The one with the huge bosom,' I say and point precisely at her.

He darts at my finger like a cat.

'What are you doing? Have you gone crazy? She's the wife of one of my best collectors.'

I try not to stop and think about the sudden pink haze that has enveloped his voice and reply, 'Well, I think the best piece in your gallery is made of flesh and blood.'

Dante giggles contentedly, but I really don't think he's happy about my behaviour. If Sveva had been in his place, how paternal I would have been!

'Don't worry,' I say quickly, 'I was joking.'

Which isn't true, but I don't want to embarrass my son. In fact, I wish that he, just once in his life, would embarrass me. But I realize that this business is pretty complicated.

'Come on,' he says a moment later and takes my arm. 'I want to introduce you to the artist, a great friend of mine.'

He leads me to the other side of the room and plonks me in front of the man with the beige jacket and the top hat. I look first at him, then at my son.

At last I ask, 'Is this the artist?'

Dante nods proudly and introduces me to Leo Perotti, the sociable man I escaped from with a hackneyed excuse; he still has the same calm, confident expression on his face. If all it took to be content with life was the ability to paint, I'd sign up for a course, but I fear that for some the beauty they encounter as adults doesn't erase the foulness they've been carrying inside them since childhood.

Perotti shakes my hand and says, 'I'm glad you didn't say you hated the painting!'

'Hmm,' I say. 'But don't you worry – if I'd thought it, I'd have said it.'

'Quite right,' Perotti replies. 'Sincerity helps us to live a better life!'

I would love to flee this sterile discussion, but Dante grips my arm more tightly than the situation requires, as if we were on a subway train with no handles to hold on to. He is agitated, I notice, because he keeps closing his eyes tightly, a tic he's retained from childhood. Very handy for a father. A simple lie was enough to bring it into the open. I remember that Caterina wanted to take him to a specialist. That's what they called them in those days – the word 'psychologist' didn't exist, or if it did it was considered too 'strong'. If you dragged your son to see a psychologist, it meant he was mad, there was little to be done. A different matter if you took him to a specialist. Dante went to neither. And this is the result.

I don't know how to continue the conversation into which I have been catapulted in spite of myself. Unfortunately I have to accept that with Dante I can't be myself; I never know what to say or do.

Sveva comes over and takes my free arm. I don't know whether my children think I'm so doddery that I can't stand up, or whether they are the ones in need of support.

'Dad, I'm off. Do you want a lift?'

Good old Sveva, turning up just in time!

I say goodbye to Dante and his excessively cordial friend and leave with her.

'Thanks for rescuing me,' I say as she turns on the ignition.

'You really are a grumpy old sod. Dante was so handsome, the exhibition was brilliant and the artist is really good. You should be proud of your son!'

'And who says I'm not?'

'Then you don't show it.'

'That's right. I don't show it because I don't know how.'

'That's what you like to think – it's easier that way.'

I press the back of my neck against the headrest and half close my eyes. I start getting a headache at the very thought of engaging in a conversation with my daughter. She, luckily, looks at the road and doesn't open her mouth, even if the rage pulsing through her is apparent in the sudden movements with which she indicates or changes gear. I have many shortcomings, but I think I'm a peaceful man; I don't anger easily, or lose my temper at the drop of a hat. With Sveva, it's as if she's furious with the whole world. I think it's because of the discussion about sincerity that I just began with that nice, gay artist. Yes, he's gay too, like many of the people at the exhibition. At any rate, as I was saying, Sveva isn't very sincere with herself, so she accumulates repression and rage. And there's not much to be done about it. For the body, rage is like excrement: a useless residue that needs to be expelled. I'm an excellent laxative for my daughter.

'Why don't you change your job?' I ask after a while.

She turns round, her face more tense than before. 'Why should I change my job?'

'To be happier.'

I expect another explosion of rage, but Sveva smiles. At least she still knows how to surprise an old man who no longer knows how to surprise himself.

'Dad, you've always found everything easy. You're unhappy? Change your job, your husband, your children. But things aren't as easy as you suggest.'

'You're young. When you get old and work out how little time you have left, you want it to be easy to change things!'

She doesn't reply.

I focus on the road and think about Dante and how wretched I feel after I've seen him. For me, Dante is like the mirror in Rossana's bedroom, ruthlessly reflecting my imperfections.

'And your brother,' I say after a while. 'Do you think he's happy?'

'What are all these questions about happiness?'

'I'd like to see you contented.'

'No, that's not true. You're feeling guilty.'

Yes, she's right. Sveva is a hard nut. She isn't afraid of me as her brother is. And she's a lawyer – unmasking lies is part of her job.

'Anyway, don't worry. In spite of your defects we made it through,' she goes on and taps me on the leg.

'You're always kind.'

'If you don't want people to tell you things, don't ask questions. You've always been silent and contented. Try and keep it that way...'

We're there. It's time for me to get out.

'And yet I think he's contented with life,' she adds at last.

'Why won't he tell me he's gay?'

'Not that old thing again? Don't draw me into affairs that don't concern me!'

Then she plants a kiss on my cheek. It's her way of saying that I've got to get out of the car. I've already closed the door when I knock on the window with my knuckles. I wait for her to wind down the window and lean into the car.

'Tell me the truth: is that friendly artist who paints Superman in a miniskirt his partner?'

'Bye, Dad,' she says and winds up the window. Then she leaves.

Yes, he's his partner.

I open the front door and call the lift. If nothing else, Leo Perotti is nice and good-humoured. Those qualities would have been enough to make Caterina happy. I imagined a very different kind of daughter-in-law. But I'm not complaining – at least he's not bald and hairy.

Chapter Thirteen
I Have Failed

Some lives are linear, and others have twists and turns. Mine certainly falls under the latter category. Only a few times have I really known what I wanted and how to get it, and the rest I've always played by ear. Even in my youth I worked out that to fulfil a dream you have to be prepared to sacrifice something, even if it's only free time, and I've never wanted to deprive myself of anything – certainly not free time.

Many of my school friends ended up doing what they believe in, and what their families wanted too. My parents had no big dreams for me, not least because I don't think they had many dreams left themselves: they had all been realized by my two big brothers. So that now I regret not having had a professional life worthy of the name, but I mustn't pick arguments with the ghosts of people who aren't around any more. Even if it would be easier. On the contrary, my failed career is entirely down to my lack of staying power. My father had been a manual worker all his life, and the day I graduated he turned up in a black jacket a size too big for him, which fell from his thin shoulders like a shawl on an old grandmother. After I got my degree he never asked anything of me, content with the little that I had given him. Then I was satisfied with the accountant's diploma that I had in my pocket and went off in search of a job, which wasn't too difficult in the mid 1950s. An uncle of my mother's had a trading office in Mergellina: it was there that I served my apprenticeship, there that I worked out that accounting wasn't the job for me, so I said goodbye to my uncle and left.

Even then my parents didn't say anything. Just as they raised no objections when I was taken on by a shoemaking business, where at first I had the job of moving the shoes from the warehouse to the shop and vice versa. Then, at a certain point, the owner, who had somehow – I never knew how – found out about my degree, asked me to keep the company's accounts in order. I resisted for ten months, and then one evening – it was Christmas – I suddenly felt short of breath and turned as red as a chilli pepper. Sitting next to me was the owner's daughter, who had recently come to help her father and at whom I had set my cap. I don't know if the panic attack (which was at the time simply called 'an indis-position') was down to my return to the world of numbers and sums, or the presence of the young woman who seemed to want to trap me in a life in which everything was preor-dained. I got up and fled without a word.

For a short while I also worked as a private investigator. It was funny, part of my job involved tailing unfaithful wives. Except that job didn't last long either. After spying on women, I fell in love with one of them. Our passion was as short-lived as it was intense, like the ravings of my boss when he fired me. At the end of our relationship I had, in fact, confessed my true identity to my lover.

In short, for years I wandered from one job to another just to keep from putting down roots and being enslaved to the idea of a mediocre but secure future. Then I met Caterina. She was a secretary at Volpe, the trading company where I had ended up through the intercession of one of my brothers. He was so happy to have helped me that I didn't have the courage to refuse the offer, even though from the first day I knew that the company wasn't going to be my future. In fact, I stayed there for the rest of my life – long enough to conquer Caterina, marry her, give her two children and then direct my attention at other women.

I fell in love straight away, the first time I saw her. She was pretty, shy but resolute, elegant, always available and welcoming. That's the exact term: Caterina knew how to welcome people, at least at first. And I have always been attracted to people who allowed me to absorb their love without laying claim to anything else.

During those years I returned to accountancy, I spent my days doing the accounts, looking for the house where we would live, the furniture we would put in it. Then, eventually, I decided to stop. I couldn't go on, I hated that job, I hated maths, I hated numbers and I hated rotting away behind a desk. I hated my life, which, once more, I hadn't chosen.

For a whole lifetime I tried to flee a sedentary job and I failed. For a whole life I kicked out, thinking I might be able to escape a fate that seemed to want to trip me up. I failed. For a whole lifetime I changed tack several times to avoid ending up as an accountant. I failed.

Anyway, during that time Caterina was very close to me. She understood my state of mind and encouraged me to find the right path. I convinced myself that I loved her a lot, even though I knew already that I no longer felt anything for her, and I threw myself into the search for a job more in harmony with my way of being. Then came the news: Caterina was pregnant. So she had to leave the company, and I had to go back. Accountancy had grabbed me once again with its long tentacles. Obviously it wasn't Caterina's fault, except that unconsciously I blamed her and her belly. Because of her pregnancy I was forced to abandon for ever my rebellious impulse – it was my wife's fault that I would lead a life I didn't want. That was when I began to hate her. Sveva was still in her womb and I was a bad husband.

I was an accountant for forty years. Work for me was something secondary, like background music. My real life was elsewhere: my children, my lovers, impossible loves, friends and dreams that always stayed as dreams and turned over the years to regret. And yet now I know that you can't treat work like something you leave to one side, because work doesn't stay on one side. I wouldn't have done many of the stupid things with which I tried to give a meaning to life if I had had an involving job.

Passion doesn't make you love your wife, it doesn't teach you to enjoy parenthood to the full, it doesn't even help you shake off the dust that has built up behind you since childhood, that's true, but at least it helps you to close your eyes in the evening and not to flounder in torment. I have spent my life lamenting Caterina, my job, my lack of freedom, the wrong choices I've made, the children who robbed me of my energy, passing time, to avoid looking in the face the one true fact: I wasn't able to change anything.

Perhaps I'm not as strong as I want to make people think.

Chapter Fourteen

The Mind

Every time I knock on Marino's door I wait for ten minutes for him to come and open up. By now he struggles even to get out of his damned armchair. He slithers like a snail to the door and at last he confronts the double-locked door. Because Marino, among other things, is paranoid about thieves slipping into his flat. To steal what, God alone knows. But the stubborn old git won't hear a word on the subject, so I wait for the key to make a complete turn in the lock and allow it to open. A few more precious seconds wasted because of someone else's obsessions. One of these days I should try and tell him that living in constant fear of danger doesn't make it go away – it just means throwing away another day of your own life. But I think that, alas, it would be a waste of time and breath.

'Marino, you can't go on locking yourself away as if you lived in a bank vault.' I guess from the expression on his face that he doesn't see the joke. But anyway, after a certain age you can't be fussy – you have to make do with the few people left by your side. I walk ahead of him into the sitting room and sit down on the sofa. Marino joins me, dragging his feet, and sinks into the armchair; the scene makes me think of a frightened snail withdrawing into its shell.

'So?' he asks. 'How's it going? Anything new?'

I can't erase from my mind the image of the enormous snail talking to me and asking questions. I'm forced to close my eyes and open them again.

'Lots,' I say. 'I've met Emma.'

'Yes, I know.'

'You know?'

'Eleonora keeps me up to date.'

'The cat lady?'

'The cat lady.'

'Nosy old bag,' I reply irritably.

He smiles, amused. There's a great gap between Marino's body and his mind. He's a bit deaf, it's true, but he's still intelligent. Often his body doesn't go the same way as his brain, so much so that one day he'll find himself in front of the mirror and won't recognize himself.

'What did she tell you?'

'That we need to do something for the girl and that you're an old grump and you wouldn't hear of it.'

'She said that? That I'm an old grump?'

'Verbatim,' he replies. 'But what *has* happened?'

I can't tell whether he was happier because Eleonora called me grumpy or old. I opt for the second hypothesis; uncomfortable truths are less frightening if they also apply to other people.

'Emma's row is in the past. She slept at mine the other night.'

Marino opens his eyes wide, grips the arms of the armchair and pulls himself to his feet.

'What did you think I meant?'

'You tell me.'

I don't know whether to get angry about the obscene thought that's whirling around in his brain, or be proud because he thinks I'm still capable of seducing a girl in her thirties.

'She knocked on my door and told me everything. She told me that the bastard has been abusing her for three years and she doesn't have the courage to get away. And she has no one here in the city. Her husband wasn't coming home, so she asked me if she could stay. She needs attention and a bit of humanity.'

Marino lets go of the arm of the chair and sinks back among the cushions.

'And what did you say to her?'

'What did I say to her? That if she doesn't report him, I will. But she begged me not to.'

'So? Aren't we going to write that threatening letter?'

I'm glad that Marino feels like an integral part of the investigation; the problem is that I don't think I'm enjoying myself as much as I was at the start. When other people's pain gets too close, you start noticing a pang of your own.

'We'll write it – why not? Even if it doesn't save her, at least we won't just be sitting on our hands. Maybe next time the bastard will think twice before hitting her.'

'Then I need to show you something,' he says with an odd little smile on his face.

I wait for him to leave his shell and follow him into the next room, where the computer is waiting for us.

'Have you talked to Orazio? Is he coming to help us?'

'Help us? We don't need any help! Shut up and look, doubting Thomas!'

Having said that, he walks over to the computer and, with slow but certain movements, he turns it on. Then he sits down at the screen and waits. When the computer is ready, I see him moving the mouse around for a few seconds, and as

if by magic a white sheet appears in front of us, ready to be
soiled by our precarious threats.

'Hey, how did you manage that?'

'I repeated the operation with my grandson for a whole
afternoon,' he answers proudly.

'Brilliant!' I say and clap him on his shoulder.

'Hey, Cesare, gently, now!'

Sometimes I forget that I'm surrounding myself with
people who are closer to that side than this. But I'm proud
of him: in his own small way he has committed himself and
wasted hours on a woman he doesn't even know. A little
gesture that no one will ever see, and which acquires even
greater value precisely because of that.

'So,' he begins, 'dictate. I'm ready!'

'You're writing?' I ask, alarmed.

'Why? Do you want to do it?'

'No. It's more that I haven't yet thought about what to say.'

'You're the brains,' Marino hurries to reply, shifting all the
responsibility for the operation on to my shoulders.

'So...write...'

The old man already has his hands ready to fall on the
keyboard, like a pianist who's just about to launch into a piece,
when the bell rings. We freeze and exchange a worried glance.

'They've found us!' he whispers.

'Are you mad? We haven't even started yet!'

'So who is it?' he asks faintly.

'What do I know? Go and open the door – it's your house!'

Marino obeys and walks fearfully away. It's just as well he
was a boy during the war – he'd have been a rotten soldier.
It's hard to imagine him in a unit of storm troopers.

As soon as he opens the door, I hear the unmistakable
voice of Signora Vitagliano. A few seconds later, the stench
arrives in the little room. It's as if the cat lady always walked

around with a collection of dead cats in her coat pocket. I hear her chatting with Marino down the corridor.

'Eleonora has come to check how things are going,' Marino tells me when they come into the room.

Perfect, now we're really a fine group of desperate people. The old man takes a chair and invites his guest to sit down, then goes back to the computer.

'So...' I say, trying to pick up the thread. 'Write: *We wan-ted to warn you that we are a-ware of the fact that you are a-bus-ing your wife. If this be-hav-iour con-tin-ues, we will be forced in spite of our-selves to a-lert the rel-e-vant au-thor-it-ies.*'

A quarter of an hour and a couple of pints of sweat later, we place the full stop. I have no more ideas, but I think it could go well.

'Have you finished already?' Eleonora shrieks.

'Well, yes, I think so,' I reply uncertainly.

'It's not right!' she exclaims vigorously.

'What's not right about it?'

'It's too soft – we need something else! Marino, write this: *You arsehole, we know you're hitting your wife. If it happens one more time, we're coming to break both your legs. You've been warned!*'

I look at the cat lady in disbelief.

Marino laughs behind his moustache as he finishes tapping out the threat.

'Gentlemen, we need serious intimidation. We want the bastard to be shitting himself. Forget the relevant authorities!'

Marino looks at me.

I reply with a nod, meaning that he is to talk and say what he thinks.

'I actually think Eleonora might have a point.'

I turn and study the old woman whose chin now rests on the back of her hands, which are clutching her trusty walking stick. The years have turned her into a witch, but one who knows what she's doing. I like her. Like Rossana and all the women who don't submit to life.

'OK, you're in the majority. Let's leave the text like that.'

'And now?' Marino asks. 'What do we do?'

'Print it, then slip the letter in the mailbox and let's see what happens.'

Marino is looking at me, perplexed.

'What is it?'

'No one's taught me how to do it…'

'Do what?'

'Print.'

'Bollocks,' I curse, before realizing I'm in the presence of a lady. But luckily the old woman didn't hear a thing and is still looking at us with a moronic smile on her face.

'Do *you* know how to do it?' Marino asks me.

'No, my relationship with technology stops with the remote control.'

'Then we'll just have to wait for my grandson Orazio. I'll call him tonight and tell him to come back.'

I snort. It's taking us days to write and deliver a letter, while out there things are taking just a few hours to go to the bad.

I take my leave of the gang and go upstairs.

There's a bag hanging from the door handle. I open it and find a tablecloth inside.

I go into my flat and read the note that accompanies the gift. It's from Emma.

So that next time you listen to what I have to tell you instead of looking for the tablecloth! PS thank you.

I turn the note around in my hands and discover that I'm very moved. As ever, it just takes a woman to bring me down.

Chapter Fifteen

Hamburger with Provolone

As far as I remember, the last time I had any kind of date I still had my driving licence. For two days now, I've been trying in vain to come up with a valid excuse, but my new sincerity doesn't help me; it seems to me that nothing counts for anything compared to the disappointment in my lover's voice. Lying to Rossana doesn't seem like a great idea to me. If she decided not to see me any more, I'd be stuffed. I'd have to find myself another lover, although she wouldn't behave like a lover and let me sleep beside her or make myself an omelette in her kitchen. And anyway I'm not sure it would be that easy.

Now I find myself waiting outside the block, like a schoolboy on his first date. Although I think a schoolboy would feel much more at ease. I have a problem: I've never socialized with Rossana outside of our lubricious encounters; I don't know how she usually dresses; if she wears heels, a hat, fur; if she puts on make-up. She might turn up wearing dungarees, or a leopard-skin cape and fishnets. If that were so, I'd pretend I didn't know her and disappear down the first dark alley.

I didn't have to ask her out – our relationship has worked just fine for two years – but now things are getting complicated. The truth is that I know her body by heart and nothing whatsoever about her character. Or at least, only one version of it. And I'm worried about discovering that I'm not going to like the other variations.

Now I'm trying to distract myself and dedicate myself to the empty road that snakes up the hill. I exhale and light myself a cigarette. This is another of the things I'd forgotten when you see a woman: all that waiting. And, well, patience isn't one of my many virtues. I hate waiting: it makes me nervous, I chain-smoke and my legs start hurting. It was one of the reasons I used to row with Caterina. I would have been ready for ages while she was still putting on her skirt, so I'd go down to the doorway and light myself a cigarette, which would turn into two or three, depending on the length of the delay. When she turned up at last, my good humour had more or less evaporated, so I would always find some reason to provoke her at the first opportunity. Often she didn't even answer, but when she decided to fight back we would argue and it spoiled the date. I ruined quite a lot of evenings for my wife. Thinking about it, I ruined them for me too. Once, the year before she died, she asked me to take her to Starita, a famous pizzeria in Materdei. The problem was that there were already dozens of people chatting as they waited for a table, and to get in you had to wait for at least forty-five minutes, more than I could spare. So I said I absolutely refused to stay under any circumstances and strode huffily away. She came breathlessly after me with a long face, and for the rest of the evening (spent in a lousy dive not far away, where we consumed a lousy pizza), she didn't address a word to me.

I look at my watch: I've been down here for fifteen minutes, and my rage is starting to become uncontrollable. There isn't much to be done about this – I don't often emerge victorious from the battle with myself to become a bit less crabby. I'm almost sure that by the time Rossana shows up, I won't be able to hide my fury and will ruin the evening.

And then she steps out of the front door and she's absolutely beautiful, impeccable, with a nice long coat that covers her legs and the heels on her shoes aren't too high. I look at her, enchanted, and I feel as if I'm seeing her for the first time. She's another Rossana, different from the one I had got to know.

I walk towards her with a hint of a smile and become aware that I'm not the only one who's embarrassed. And yet we're adults, we're grown-ups; we should be more self-assured. The fact is that we've done everything backwards – we went first to bed, then to dinner – and at our age it's hard to accept that some things are simply common sense. For some reason I don't usually think about Rossana's job, but this evening I don't think I can forget it.

'How are you?' she says.

'Fine, thank you. Shall we take a taxi?'

'Is it far?'

'Twenty minutes' walk.'

'Then let's walk, so you can tell me something about yourself.'

Her new role hasn't made her shake off her usual candour. A point in her favour.

'Why? Don't you know me well enough? You know more about me than my kids do.'

She looks at me smugly and slips her arm under mine. Now we really look like an old couple who have decided to go out to boost a rotten marriage.

'You know me better than anyone.'

'Your best customer,' I observe with a half-smile.

She grows serious. 'No, I don't go to dinner with my customers,' she replies eventually.

'*So what am I?*' I want to ask her, but I'm scared of what the answer might be.

'I managed to get the name of my son's employer and the address of the shop,' she says after a moment's silence.

'Well done. I'll jot them both down later, so we can go and have a word with this "gentleman".'

Her face brightens. She's happy, and she isn't trying to hide it. If only inviting a woman to dinner was enough to make you feel right. But I'm under no illusions: you might be smiling, joking, speaking impeccable Italian, rounding the evening off brilliantly, but it doesn't erase the sense of inadequacy that you carry around with you. Rossana is one of those people who need an excuse to live, as if their mere existence might be irritating somebody.

We walk slowly, and every now and again she peers into the windows of the closed shops. I can't help thinking it might have been a good idea to take a taxi, not least because a motorbike behind us honks its horn. I turn instinctively and find myself facing two young lads with Mohicans, cigarettes dangling from their lips and necks covered with tattoos. They look at me with a rude expression that clashes with their youthful faces. They want some room on the pavement. The problem is that I have no desire to comply, so I don't move. Then one of them says, 'Let me past, grandpa. Shift your arse!'

Rossana grips my arm in a pointless bid to make me keep my temper.

'Apart from the fact that I'm not your grandpa, I don't know if you've noticed, but this is a pavement!'

But they don't even answer, and slip the nose of the motorcycle into the only available gap between me and my companion. A moment later they have disappeared into the many labyrinths of the Spanish Quarter behind us. A shame – I was anticipating their gaping jaws when they heard the speech I was going to give them. I was planning on being the retired cop this time.

'Are you determined to get beaten up?' Rossana asks me.

'They wouldn't have done that. And anyway, I can't keep my mouth shut.'

'It's not a good idea to act the hero in this city. Haven't you worked that one out yet?'

'And yet this is the place where they really need heroes, not in Milan or Turin.'

She smiles bitterly and says, 'And yet they didn't really think you were one.'

'It's true, but if I only ever opened my mouth when I was sure someone was listening, I'd be mute for the rest of my days.'

Rossana giggles and slips her arm into mine again. 'How was your son's exhibition?' she asks, determined to return to our evening together.

'Great. He was happy with it.'

'What about you? Were you OK?'

'Well, the canapés weren't bad.'

'Idiot. I meant, did you spend some time with your children?'

'With Sveva, yes. Dante was busy tending to his beloved collectors.'

'Don't talk like that.'

'It's the truth.'

'How's your daughter?' she asks.

'Neurotic.'

She stops and stares at me. 'Cesare, can you say anything nice about your family?'

Well, in fact, I find it really hard. A father doesn't usually notice a child's shortcomings, whereas those are *all* I notice.

'The truth is that she really gets on my nerves. She's an unhappy woman who doesn't realize that she is.'

'It isn't easy. Perhaps she just needs some help.'

'As if! Like my neighbour who's getting beaten up by her husband.'

Rossana looks at me with eyes made enormous by mascara, then replies, 'And what do you know about it?'

'I hear them, and I've met her. I've also told her I want to help her, but she's not having it.'

'Sorry, what does this have to do with Sveva?'

'It does have something to do with her. No one can be saved if they don't want to be. And Sveva doesn't.'

Rossana snorts. 'You spend too much time on your own,' she observes after a while.

'Why? What makes you think that?'

'Because you're a bit too direct.'

I laugh. Caterina used to say pretty much the same thing.

'And here's where my daughter works,' I say, pointing to the door of Sveva's office.

Rossana looks at the building and observes, 'She must be an important lawyer to have an office bang in the middle of town. You should be proud of her.'

'I am,' I say, noticing a detail that captures my attention from the corner of my eye, 'but not so much because of her work as because she earns respect. In some ways she resembles me.'

'Then she's got a horrible personality,' Rossana jokes, but I'm not even listening – I'm still focused on the detail I've just noticed.

I wonder whether it's time to turn back, but then decide not to ruin my companion's evening and I change the subject.

'So, why are you here with me?' I ask.

'In what sense?'

'What do you really think of me? You've never told me.'

Rossana pauses for a moment before continuing. 'I think you're a beautiful person who's doing everything he can to seem ugly.'

That's why I go out with Rossana, why I take her to dinner and spend more time with her than I do with my grandson: she throws the truth in my face without too many qualms.

'Well, let's just say that that's how people who are fond of me prefer to see things.'

'And who says I'm fond of you?' she asks ironically.

'It's obvious. Otherwise you wouldn't have come to bed with me,' I whisper. 'My appearance isn't exactly my strong point!'

She laughs.

I think that however hard I try, I still can't get that detail that I noticed outside Sveva's office out of my head.

'Listen,' I say at last, 'I've got to go back and check something. Do you mind? It'll only take five minutes.'

'What is it?' she says.

'Just a stupid thing. But if I don't go and see, it's going to gnaw away at me.'

Rossana lets me drag her back without putting up too much resistance. When we're back below my daughter's office, the detail is still there.

'You see that car?' I turn to Rossana, pointing at an SUV in front of me.

'Which one?'

'The big dark one parked below Sveva's office.'

'Yes,' she says hesitantly.

'I may be mistaken, but it looks to me like the same car I spotted her in the other day, with a man.'

Rossana stares at me for a second or two, while I dedicate myself to the SUV without taking my eyes off it, like a cat, neck craned and ears pricked, barely moving. I've always been impressed by the way animals can concentrate for minutes at a time, waiting for a single movement, however small. While sometimes you can't even attract the attention of a human being with a slap in the face.

'And do you see the light on up there? That's Sveva's office.'

'So?' she asks, after what seems to me like an endless pause.

'So that might be the same car and he might be up there with her.'

Rossana laughs. It doesn't seem to me that there's anything amusing about my hypothesis.

'This is a part of you I didn't know. You're paranoid.'

Do you know how many other parts of me you haven't known? Under the sheets, you only discover a man's minor defects.

'I prefer to say that I'm far-sighted. My daughter is having an extramarital affair!'

'Because she was in a car with a guy?'

'There's also the fact that the phantom guy rested his hand on her thigh when he was saying goodbye to her. I don't think that if you give a colleague or a friend a lift you get to touch their leg as a reward. Otherwise the whole city would be full of perverts offering women lifts.'

Rossana is still amused; my words seem to put her in a good mood. While I am extremely serious, and take my phone and call Sveva.

'What on earth are you doing?' Rossana asks.

I don't reply, not least because the phone is already ringing.

'Dad.'

'Hi, Sveva. How are you?'

'I'm well, why?'

She sounds breathless.

Rossana comes over to my ear to listen.

'So, I wanted to know everything was all right.'

She says nothing for a moment, then replies uneasily, 'Of course, everything's fine.'

'You sound strange, agitated.'

'What do you mean? I'm not used to you calling and asking me questions all the time, the way you've been doing over the past few days.'

I'm actually behaving like a demented old fool who no longer has a life of his own and is trying to nose his way into his children's lives.

'I just wanted to say hello. Where are you? At home?'

'What? Yes, I'm at home.'

Her voice betrays her insecurity. I know my daughter. I know that she's not easily overwhelmed, but when it happens she doesn't know how to defend herself and surrenders to the enemy, like a vulnerable puppy with the leader of the pack. But I'm not going to have pity on her – I want to go all the way.

'Pass me Federico. I'd like to say hello.'

Silence again.

'Dad, this isn't the time. He has to have a bath and go to bed. I'll call you tomorrow, sorry.' And she hangs up before I can say anything.

I turn towards Rossana, who is looking at me curiously.

'My daughter is feeding me a pack of lies,' I observe, and slip the phone back into my jacket.

'That's normal. All children do that,' she says, trying to soften the blow.

'I'm sure she's up there with her lover.'

'And what if she is? What can you do about it? It's her life.'

It's exactly what I would have said to a friend – to Marino, for example, who has the terrible habit of poking his nose into his daughter's life. Just as I'm doing now.

The light in the room goes out.

I grab Rossana's arm, while she goes on dispensing advice that I'm not listening to, and drag her behind a van. She looks at me as if I'm crazy. *I'm not crazy, dear Rossana. I'm a quick-change artist, I told you. Now I'm playing the part of detective.*

'Cesare, I don't want to go along with this. Spying on your daughter just seems out of order!'

If only you knew how many other things I do every day that are out of order, my dear Rossana. Even continuing to leave money on your bedside table seems a bit out of order to both of us, and yet you don't have anything to say about that.

'One moment, and then we'll be on our way,' I reply, careful not to take my eyes off the entrance to the building.

'It's getting late…' she tries to counter.

The electric hum of the door precedes Sveva's exit. I open my eyes wide. By her side there is a distinguished man in his sixties, with white hair and a belly pressing against his shirt. They look cautiously around before climbing into the SUV, which opens with a beep.

I hear Rossana beside me, whispering, 'You were right…'

The car reverses and sets off.

All of a sudden I couldn't care less about dinner, about Rossana and the fact that I'm not going to make love ever again in my lifetime. I grip my companion by the arm and run to the taxi rank at the end of the street.

'What are you doing?' she wails, clutching her handbag.

'We've got to follow them!'

'You're crazy!'

Yes, I'm crazy, but you should have noticed that before. You've had two years to notice, my girl, and now it's too late, and if you don't shift your arse we'll lose the SUV and we can kiss the pursuit goodbye.

I stop a taxi and tell the driver to tail the car. We get in.

I'm breathless, and can barely speak, but I've still got to apologize to Rossana: 'I'm sorry for ruining your evening, but I need to know what my daughter's up to.'

She doesn't reply, so I turn to the taxi driver to ask him to go faster. The man mutters something and accelerates very slightly. Our car chase clearly doesn't mean anything to him. At a red light he stops a moment before the SUV gets away.

I lean forward and shout, 'What are you doing? Go on, keep going!'

He turns round and shoots back rudely: 'Listen, I don't care what you're up to, but I'm not getting a fine!'

At this point I feel the need to do my quick-change act. 'Perhaps you don't recognize me. I'm the chief inspector of police and I'm following a criminal. I order you to jump the red light, or tomorrow your licence will be so much waste paper!'

He turns pale, takes off his cloth cap and says, 'I'm sorry, chief inspector, I didn't recognize you.'

Then he turns round, puts the car in first and screeches away. A few moments later we are behind our prey.

Rossana smiles at last, and I smile back. She was the right choice: she might sell her body for money, but she's the only one who's amused by my acts of idiocy. And at my age you need a woman who makes you think you're still an agreeable person and not an old sod to be abandoned in an armchair in front of the TV.

The car stops a few blocks from Sveva's house. She and her companion speak, kiss, then at last she gets out and walks off. I find myself thinking about how, in a few minutes, she will be with Diego and Federico, and what she will do to cover up the deception. I thought I was being good in a way, but maybe I wasn't; perhaps children have paranormal powers, and the mask we're still wearing when we come home from work fails to materialize in front of their eyes. So we think we're shielded, when in fact we're naked. I see myself in Sveva. I betrayed her mother; she's betraying her husband.

The taxi driver looks at me. I think he wants to know what we're doing, but I'm the chief inspector and he's too respectful of my role to ask any questions.

'Follow that car,' I say in the austere voice that one uses when addressing official employees.

Rossana darts me another glance, the umpteenth this evening, and I nod, as if to say that I have the situation under control. The taxi driver is sweating and he's clearly worried – perhaps he thinks he's tailing a powerful Camorra boss rather than an old man with a paunch and a vulgar car. In my day they had Fiat 500s, which you had to bend over to drive if you were too tall, whereas now they're like ocean liners and God only knows what the point of them is. The world is getting smaller every day, and yet we go on producing bigger and bigger things.

But now I'm facing a different set of problems. For example, I've spent the last ten minutes wondering why Sveva prefers to spend her precious time in the arms of a dirty old man rather than at home with her husband and Federico. Then I work it out. A woman seeks outside of marriage what she doesn't find inside it: Diego is a great guy, but he's too good, like Marino. I've already said what I think about good people. It means that the individual we're following specializes in villainy, and I can't allow my daughter to fall into the clutches of a perfidious man, however pleasant, confident, cheerful and jovial he might be. She's already got me for all that.

'What do you plan to do?' Rossana whispers.

'I don't know.'

I do know, in fact, except I'm no longer quite so sure. What right do I have in the end to make decisions on behalf of my daughter? Haven't I done the same thing? But the question that's bouncing around in my brain is a different one: am I actually sure that it's better to spend your life beside a good but boring man rather than one who's nice but selfish? Evil can lurk behind even the most affable of faces. Except that I'm involved now, and I need to know something more about the old man who's taking Sveva to bed. And there I was, worrying about Dante's sexual proclivities! That chatty artist is a fashion model in comparison.

The SUV stops on the seafront. The man turns on the hazard lights, gets out of the car and goes into a tobacconist's. When he comes out, he has a cigar in his mouth and a bag full of colourful objects. I lean forward to see more clearly, and realize that they are those little plastic animals that children like so much, including my grandson. Once I bought him a box containing a fence, some pigs, a few dappled cows and some sheep. Federico played with it long enough to build the fence and put the animals inside to graze. A few days later the cheerful little farm lay sadly in a bag along with a thousand other toys that had ceased to fulfil their function, a bit like those cars that rot in the fields beside motorways.

The man gets back into the car and sets off again. I look around. We're a long way from our restaurant, following a person who, apart from having a relationship with my daughter, must have some grandchildren dotted about the city. Maybe he's not as bad as all that. Maybe it's not always right to say that you seek something different outside of marriage. Maybe some people just feel the need to rediscover themselves through a new face, a different perfume, eyes that look at you with curiosity.

'Fine, just drop us off here!' I say, surrendering.

The taxi driver sighs with relief, as if he had escaped a serious danger, and gives me yet another free ride, one of the many I've had in my life.

'You're really something, you know that?' Rossana observes.

We've missed that romantic dinner. I've ruined our evening over a fit of teenage jealousy, and now she's going to tell me to bugger off.

'And yet I've never enjoyed a first date so much in my life!' she carries on delightedly, to my surprise.

What a woman. Rossana, if I were ten years younger I'd marry you! We hug and find ourselves standing facing one another once again, our mouths only a few inches apart. I come to my senses and move away. I can't kiss her – not now, not here, when there are people around. If someone called the police over indecent acts in a public place, I wouldn't be able to deny it.

'I'm sorry. It's just that seeing my daughter with a man like that has put my nerves on edge.'

'Don't worry, I quite understand,' she says. 'As a matter of fact, I don't know what she sees in that old man.'

'Thanks for the compliment!'

'Don't be stupid. I meant old from her point of view.'

I look around. In front of us there's a van selling panini. An idea comes to mind.

'How about I buy you a delicious morsel from that stall over there?'

She turns round and bursts out laughing, then takes my hand and links my fingers with hers. And, incredibly, a shiver darts along my arm and melts away behind my back. I think the last woman with whom I engaged in such intimacy was my wife. My rough, mottled hands are now more used to grabbing a buttock than touching someone else's palm. Advancing age inexorably devours the little poetry that still flickers in my belly.

I treat her to a hamburger with provolone, and I have a hot dog with sauerkraut – not exactly ideal for a first romantic date. But there hasn't been very much romance at all this evening, just Rossana lifting up her coat a little before sitting on the low wall along the road. I do the same, then take a long sip from the bottle of ice-cold Peroni and hand it to her. Behind us the still sea reflects the lights of the villas of Posillipo, where people my age dine on silver platters with servants standing behind them. Meanwhile I drink straight from the bottle and if I could I would allow myself a loud burp that would ease the turmoil in my stomach.

'And yet this evening I worked out that my son is in good hands,' she says eventually. 'If Sveva is anything like you, as you say she is, she must be a lion in the courtroom!'

We sit on the wall for an hour, laughing about ourselves and life in general, until she reminds me that it's late and tomorrow's a working day. In a context like that, with the sea and the Castel dell'Ovo behind us, the strolling families and Vesuvius spying on us, I had forgotten I was just a bent old man. I'd forgotten that life is like this city: it's an illusion. All those lights, the smiling people, the market stalls, the carts selling candyfloss, the honking bicycles, the moon reflected in the water and casting its light on Capri in the distance are little in comparison with the silence of the many dirty and forgotten boulevards, the lament of the alleyways that sweat violence, the fearful expressions on the faces of those who haven't yet worked out how to confront the other face of the city.

We get to our feet and walk towards the taxis. The play is over – it's time to get back to reality – but I'm happy anyway. At the start of the evening I was worried that I would meet a different woman, one I didn't like, and yet I discovered that there are no other versions of Rossana; she's always the same, whether in lingerie or in a blouse or a skirt, on a mattress or on a wall. Who knows? She might even win my children over.

I'm already home when I receive a text message. It's Rossana. After countless attempts, I finally manage to read the text.

It says: *Thank you for the loveliest evening. I won't forget you!*

My eyes mist over, so I hurl the phone on the sofa and go to the bathroom. Who'd have thought that at my age I could still be moved by a woman's words?

As I sit on the toilet, my lips decide to break the silence of the flat: *'I just wanted to tell you that this evening a woman held my hand and moved me in a way that hasn't happened for ages. I know, it's not pretty of me to come and confide in you. But you're the only one I felt I could tell. Goodnight.'*

Then I pull the chain and go to bed.

It's better that I don't even mention Sveva.

Chapter Sixteen

There Are Two of Us

The light tells me that the cabin, as always, has stopped on the seventh floor. There must be some kind of cosmic magnetism, a special law of gravity that attracts the lifts to the top floor. I press the button and wait for the old box to come and get me.

A few yards up the road a door closes violently, before someone comes running down the stairs. I lean towards the lift shaft and see him, my crazy neighbour, charging down the stairs like a lunatic. My heart thumps in my chest, because the man isn't just in a hurry – he's running away. And if he's running away it's because he's hurt Emma.

I decide to confront him.

As soon as he notices that I am there, he slows down and half closes his eyes. Obviously he hasn't yet forgotten the lesson that I've taught him. A few feet away from me, he freezes and apologizes. I don't move an inch. My heart is racing, I feel dizzy and a drop of sweat trickles down my forehead. Nonetheless I don't step back. An army general wouldn't.

'Will you let me past?' he asks.

I study him. He's sweating, his hair is standing up in crazy tufts and his pupils are dilated.

'What has happened?' I manage to ask.

'What's supposed to have happened?' he says.

'Why are you running?'

'Why? Aren't you allowed to run in this block any more?'

In fact, I find it pretty difficult to come up with a sensible answer to that one.

'Where's your wife?' I ask.

He recoils only for a moment, before deciding to attack.

'And what's it to you, if you don't mind me asking?'

I feel the sweat trickling down my vest, and my vision is blurred. This is no longer a simple, innocuous joke – I'm really risking a beating here. And at my age I don't think I'd get away with a few bruises.

'It matters in a house where you're still taking the liberty of abusing her.'

There, I've said it.

He looks at me fiercely before losing control. 'Move your feet, you old tosser!' And he pushes me aside.

A moment later he's outside.

Luckily the wall supports me, so I don't collapse on the ground, unlike my shopping bag, whose contents have spilled around the hallway. *I swear you'll pay for that, you bastard!* Sure, but how?

I pull down the frame of my glasses, which has slipped up to my temples, then start picking up the goods. The building is full of people coming and going; you can't call the lift without someone rabbiting on at you about the weather while you cower in a corner. But whenever I need help, there's never anyone about.

In the end I manage to get home. I go straight to the kitchen, put the bags down on the table, take the two boxes of frozen food and put them in the freezer, then, without even taking my jacket off, I knock at Emma's door.

She opens up after what seems like a very long time. Her lip is split and she is cradling one of her arms. I look at her in alarm and for a moment my instinct tells me to go after the bastard. Then I realize it would make more sense to stay and look after her – there's plenty of time to make him pay for it.

'May I come in?' I ask.

'If he comes back he'll kill you first and then me.'

For the first time her prediction doesn't even seem all that wild: the man is a dangerous lunatic. I take her by her good wrist and push her into my flat. She doesn't resist. I turn on the light in the bathroom and clean her wounds with cotton wool and alcohol, then try to move her arm.

Emma cries out with pain.

'Did he hit you in the stomach as well?'

She just shakes her head. It's only when she sees my worried look that she adds, 'No, no, I swear. I was careful to protect it.'

Dear Christ, how can you witness all this without intervening? I don't think I can.

'We have to go to the hospital and tell the police the truth. Report that piece of crap!'

'No, please don't,' she says, bursting into tears. 'Don't do that to me!'

'Why? Why don't you want me to help you? Why are you defending him?'

'I swear I'll escape before then. But, please, don't report him. It would only make things worse…'

'I don't get it…' I whisper.

I call a taxi. When we get there I'll tell the truth, whatever happens. Even if it means Emma hating me, telling me that her life is her own, I'll do what needs to be done.

At A & E they make us wait with some other people in a

big room with only a few chairs and a lot of patients lying silently on stretchers.

We sit there in complete silence, busy looking around, and then eventually I turn to her and ask, 'How could you fall in love with a man like that?'

Emma sighs and goes on holding her arm. 'I don't know. I can't remember.'

'And why won't you let me help you?'

'Cesare, you don't understand. If we reported him this evening, we'd just have to run for it. You *and* me!'

No, I don't understand. And I never will.

'Why did he hit you this time?'

She turns away.

'You don't want to tell me?'

She answers without looking at me. 'I didn't want to make love – I was frightened for the child. And he lost it completely!'

I don't reply. I don't know what to do.

'I'm sorry for involving you,' she whispers after a few moments of silence.

'What do you mean?'

'I shouldn't have gone into your house that evening.'

'But it was a good idea.'

'Do you want to know the truth?' And she looks me straight in the eyes.

I nod.

'His ex reported him for abuse as well. The trial is ongoing.'

I shake my head and sigh.

She goes on. 'If I reported him, he'd go straight to jail!'

'And you don't want that?' I ask too loudly.

'I just want what's good for me, not what's bad for him.'

Even her swollen face and clotted blood look beautiful to

me. If I were the same age I would challenge the world just
to have her and protect her.

'How can you say such things? He nearly broke your arm!'

A tear slips down her cheek and she immediately wipes it
away with her good hand. Life has taught her not to show
pain.

'I don't want to destroy him. I just want to leave him.'

'And you don't care about the others who come after you?
Whose lives you might save through your actions?'

She turns and stares at me, her face filled with frustration.
'Do you think I haven't thought about that? That I don't ask
forgiveness every night for my lack of courage?'

Her suffering spills into the tears that are now slipping
slowly down her face. I don't know what to reply, and try to
fight back the desire to draw her to me.

After a while, her weeping subsides and Emma slumps in
her chair with a snort, like an old bus that has reached its
destination. Then she stays there, staring into the distance,
her lips parted in an attempt to get her breath back. I study
her and linger on that flaw that makes her unique, the detail
that has drawn me from the start.

'Did he break that tooth?' I ask.

She touches the incisor with her tongue. 'This one?'

'Yes.'

She smiles – the first time this evening – and says, 'No, I
broke it as a girl. I fell off my bicycle.'

'I like it,' I observe.

'You like it? My broken tooth?'

'Yes, your broken tooth.'

'You're a very strange person,' she replies, a moment
before she's called.

In the room there's a doctor sitting behind a desk; beside
him a man in a green coat clutching a folder full of papers

for him to sign. Emma and I stand there for a while, waiting for a nod. The doctor doesn't even look at us and goes on endlessly signing the papers. It's only when he's finished the last one that the doctor gets to his feet, grabs Emma's arm, tries to turn it and freezes when she screams. After that he inspects the bruises and scratches along her body.

Then he turns to me. I return his quizzical gaze until he asks, 'Who are you? Her father?'

'A friend,' I reply angelically.

The man starts becoming suspicious and, turning to Emma, continues with his questioning. 'What has happened to you?'

'I fell off my bike.'

That bike, again. I wonder if she was telling the truth before or if it's a standard excuse that she uses on every occasion. The doctor doesn't seem to believe her either, and yet he doesn't press the point, instead turning back to me.

'Is that what happened? The young lady fell?'

Emma stares at me.

Here it is, the moment to tell the truth and send her husband to jail. But her eyes are pleading with me not to speak. I lower my head. I can't defy her will – I don't have the right. I say nothing, and the doctor repeats the question.

'Yes, that's what happened,' I admit at last.

The man is becoming impatient; who knows how many times he's witnessed similar scenes. You can read in his face that he's worked out the truth and is only making his mind up how involved he should get.

'I'm expecting a baby!' Emma says suddenly.

The doctor looks at her belly and then, turning to the nurse beside him, he says abruptly, 'Fine, then let's just take an ultrasound of her abdomen and bind up that arm.'

The nurse accompanies Emma outside. I'm about to go back to the waiting room, when the man in the white coat holds me back.

'You know how many women I've seen in that state or worse? And you know almost all of them have fallen off their bikes, off a chair, a swing or a scooter?'

I lower my head. I can't hold his gaze.

'What do you want me to do?' I ask at last.

'Nothing. But if you can, persuade the lady to speak out!'

'I've done what I can. But why didn't you ask the girl these questions?'

'She would never have told me the truth.'

'That's not true. It's just what you want to think,' I reply, before leaving and going back to my seat.

Out of the corner of my eye I notice the doctor staring at me and shaking his head disapprovingly. Don't take me for a doddery old fool. We're not that different, you and me. In one way and another, we've decided not to intervene and to mind our own business. Just hope that one day we won't have to share the remorse as well.

Emma comes out half an hour later with her arm bandaged. She comes towards me and looks at me with tears in her eyes. She waits for me to speak.

'Don't worry, I didn't tell them anything.'

Her lips smile, before she puts her good arm around my shoulders.

I struggle to return the hug. But I really can't manage a smile.

Chapter Seventeen

I'd Like to Be an Orc

There are days when you want to hide the terrible truth from yourself; the years you carry around with you are obvious and as heavy as boulders. On the bus a spotty boy with headphones in his ears felt obliged to sit up as soon as I boarded, as if he were an army private and I were his sergeant major. I stared at him with hatred in my eyes, but he said, 'I insist.' At that point I was obliged to sit down, to avoid the disapproving looks of the other passengers. Yes, I know, I should have thanked him for his friendly gesture, but instead I sat down and turned my wrinkled face to the window. In fact, it was my mistake: I shouldn't have taken the bus, a concentration of people trying to outdo one another in making people feel sorry for them. I would happily break my femur to keep from prompting a similar feeling in other people.

And it didn't stop there. Afterwards it got even worse, if that's possible. I was sitting on a bench outside the school, waiting for my grandson, Federico. This time, yet again, I couldn't find a plausible excuse to get out of it. I was minding my own business when I noticed that a group of three little boys were looking at me and laughing. I looked away – after all, they were just children – and looked instead at the waiting mummies, probably a better spectacle. But those three scoundrels wouldn't stop making fun of me. *That's right, you little rogues, you just amuse yourselves*, I thought. *Just you wait till life swaps the roles and you find yourselves waiting on a bench to pick up a snotty little brat.* Then I looked down and noticed that my flies were undone, which is as funny as it gets when you're eight. I remedied the situation discreetly and turned to my three detractors with a welcoming grimace on my face, beckoning them to join me. The little things were terrified, but the biggest one came over to me.

'Hi,' I said cordially.

He answered without looking up.

'Do you know who I am?'

The young whippersnapper's hands clutched the straps of his rucksack. He looked at me and shook his head.

'I'm a policeman,' I told him, still with a smile on my face and with a persuasive voice.

His eyes opened wide.

'You know it's not nice to make fun of a policeman? It's something you really shouldn't do – your mother should have taught you that!'

He stared at the ground. When I want to, I can instil a certain fear in people.

'So what should I do now? Take you down to the station?'

At that point the little boy started crying and a lady looked over to see what was happening. Perhaps I'd overdone it, so I got up and tried to make amends.

'No, don't worry,' I said. 'Policemen are nice people. Come and let me buy you an ice cream.'

But he ran off to his friends, who, after a swift confabulation, took to their heels. Luckily no one noticed what had happened.

But the best thing was yet to come. I picked up my grandson and we walked towards his mother's office. But, as we know, an old man and a little boy can't walk for very long without needing to go for a pee. So we went into a big shop and asked for directions to the toilet. Every time I have to use a public convenience I thank God for that burden I have between my legs. If I were a woman I would wet myself rather than stand in a queue. Anyway, I helped Federico and then asked him to wait for me outside; if he had seen me sitting down to urinate, in fact, many of his certainties would have shattered in a trice.

The problem was that when I came out he wasn't there. I thought he might have gone to the exit, but I was wrong. I went back in and asked the ladies in the queue. No one had seen a little boy. I went into a cold sweat. The truth, as I've said before, is that I can't look after a grandchild; at my age people ought to be looking after me rather than the other way round. I searched the whole shop before I finally spotted him, stroking a Labrador puppy.

I went over and, still in a daze, yelled, 'Federico, what the hell are you doing? I told you not to move!'

He tried for a moment not to cry, his little mouth trembling with the effort to hold himself back, but at last he burst into tears, mortified.

The owner of the dog looked at me threateningly and said, 'What sort of manners are those?'

'You can shut up,' I replied. 'Didn't you notice that the child was on his own? Didn't it occur to you that perhaps somebody might be looking for him?'

She took a step back and said, 'How dare you?'

'Oh, I dare. Believe me, I dare,' I shot back. 'And just be grateful that I'm in a good mood today!'

I grabbed Federico by the hood of his sweatshirt and dragged him outside. For about ten minutes we didn't say a word, the boy busy holding in his tears, me chewing on my remorse. I know how to entertain a prostitute, how to pretend I'm an army general, how to silence a man who's abusing a woman; I know how to shift an old man out of his armchair and welcome into my home someone in need of refuge. But I don't know how to be a thoughtful grandpa. I'm not capable of giving love to those who have a right to it.

I was thinking these thoughts as I walked in silence. I'm still thinking them, sitting on the sofa in my daughter's office, with Federico sleeping beside me and Sveva lodging a legal appeal. I watch her and it's as if I don't recognize her. I don't understand who caused her the rancour that she hides behind. She's a brusque character, all sharp edges and tetchiness. I would never deign to look at a woman like that; I like broad curves, the kind to be approached in a low gear. Sharp bends weary me – they force you to shift up a gear or two. My daughter is like an alpine pass, a sequence of switchback turns.

'Right, I'm off,' I say, to distract her attention from the threats that she is probably vomiting out on to the keyboard.

'Wait, I've nearly finished. Shall we have lunch together?'

From bad to worse. 'OK.'

She is starting to intimidate me again, and I watch her carefully. I wonder how it's possible to spend your whole day making your fellow man pay for the misdeeds of someone else. But perhaps it's better for me – better for Sveva to give vent to her shortcomings in a courtroom rather than holding me to account.

I turn and look at my grandson. In the end I apologized, and bought him an orc, a little monster about four inches tall, to which I am grateful for stealing the show away from me. Federico actually devoted himself to his new friend and soon forgot he had a grumpy grandpa. I don't think I ever apologized to Sveva and Dante – perhaps not even to my wife. I always thought that apologies had more to do with reinforcing the rightness of the recipient than with putting events in the past. But when you're old things slip by in front of your nose and you can't afford to waste precious time on abstruse conjectures. That's why, these days, I apologize and move on.

'OK, I've finished. Let's go,' Sveva says suddenly and offers me her arm. Strangely, she's smiling.

I get up, careful not to wake Federico. I would love not to succumb to flattery and to stick my hands in my pockets, but she would take offence. Try telling her that, to an old man who's doing everything in his power not to feel old, leaning on his daughter makes him feel even older. At any rate the torment doesn't last very long, just enough to travel the length of the corridor, at the end of which Sveva guides me into the conference room.

I look around, puzzled, and ask, 'Weren't we going out for lunch?'

'Of course,' she replies with the same smile she had two minutes ago. 'We're having lunch in here.'

'Here?'

'Here,' she answers brusquely.

At that moment two female flunkeys come in clutching sheets of A4 and arrange them on the glass top of the table, making them look like napkins. I watch the horrific scene play out until Sveva invites me to sit down. A few seconds later the longed-for food arrives: tuna salad and sweetcorn and a slice of wholemeal bread.

The girls say goodbye and leave us to eat. The only people left in the office are Sveva, me and Federico, who is sleeping calmly in the other room with the orc for company. Lucky him, I would add – better a revolting monster than Sveva cranked up to the max. I think the mistake I made has been to visit my daughter only in her place of work, she might be more human and sympathetic elsewhere.

'So,' she says, 'what have you got to tell me?'

But I'm not even listening. In almost eighty years I've never eaten off a sheet of A4.

'Why do you eat like this?' I ask.

'How?' she says, surprised.

'In this barbarous way!'

'What's barbarous about a bit of salad?'

'Not the salad, using a sheet of paper as a napkin in a conference room!'

'You're getting stuffy in your old age,' she murmurs and brings the food to her mouth.

I'd like to slap her right now – her know-all airs are really making me furious.

'Sveva, you've got to stop throwing your life away! Stop thinking only about work, take a trip, throw away the horrible suits you have in your wardrobe, dress a bit younger and save your relationship with your husband!'

There, I've said it.

She stares at me with her fork suspended in mid-air, the oil from the salad dripping on to the plate. She's furious, I can tell from her eyes. When she gets angry her pupils look like a scratch in the iris, like cats' eyes. And like cats, when they're attacked, out come their claws.

'How dare you talk about my life, my work and my marriage? Who are you to tell me what I can and can't do?'

Her shrill voice makes the glass under our elbows tremble. I've ruined lunch with my own bare hands. I could have smiled slyly, made some stupid comment and disappeared, got back to my life, to my sofa, to Marino, Rossana and the other useless things with which I try to fill the void. Instead I went on the attack, and now I have to lower my helmet and advance into the battlefield.

'Who am I?' I say. 'Until I receive proof to the contrary, I'm still your father!'

'Oh no, my dear man, that's too easy. You should have thought very hard before presenting yourself as the model parent dispensing advice!'

When you know you're wrong, there are two possible paths you can take: you can beat a hasty retreat or you can attack. At least I'll let off steam.

'What have I ever deprived you of? Come on, tell me? Your brother might well be able to say something of the kind, but you certainly can't. And yet he doesn't say a word – the one doing the complaining is always you!'

She tries to calm down again. She regains her composure, picks up the napkin and wipes her mouth.

'Do you really think you were a good father?' she asks.

'No, I haven't been a good father. I've made loads of mistakes, but, you see, I think you're making plenty with Federico. You're always in that damned office. Even if I made lots of mistakes, I always tried to be there for you!'

Her fury seems to subside somewhat, although I notice that her hands are shaking when she pours herself a glass of water.

'Dad, you did a lot of stupid things, but I don't want to rake over the past forty years. I'd just like you at least to be coherent, as you have always been. If there was one good quality that I acknowledged until a few years ago, it was that. You've never advised us which route to go down, you've never helped us to choose, you've never explained how life works, but at least you've never asked for anything in return either. You were honest: you didn't give and you didn't demand.' She lowers her head.

She's right about that: I've never thought that my children owed me anything. Caterina did. Mothers often maintain that love which is given must be returned in some way. A kind of blackmail, if you like.

'Recently, though, you've changed. You judge our lives, you pronounce sentences, you give opinions and advice.'

It's old age that makes you think you know how the world works, just because you've had the good fortune to be on the planet longer than other people. That's what I should reply, and instead I say something completely different: 'It's because when I was younger I didn't notice you were unhappy. And I assure you that it was much better that way.'

'But who told you we're unhappy? What's this new fixation all about?'

I study her eyes: her pupils are round again. And that's better – it means that she's retracted her claws.

'Are you happy, Sveva?' I ask. 'Can you tell me with absolute conviction that you're contented with your life?'

She looks at her plate. 'Why? Is there anyone who can claim as much? Are you happy?'

'Yes, I'm as happy as an old man can be when he's decided to go on stealing from life for as long as he can get away with it.'

'Maybe that's easier at your age.'

Sure, it's true. It's only when you know you have no alternative that you set off down that track. Come what may.

'I saw you the other evening,' I whisper.

I know I'm making the umpteenth mistake of my life, but I'm being guided by instinct. It's always been that way – in difficult situations it nudges me out of my seat and sits down in my place. I let it get on with it, because it's much more comfortable to enjoy the scene from behind.

'Where?'

'With that man, when you were coming out of your office.'

Her face turns red, then she picks up her glass and gulps down the water. She's thinking about what she should say in reply.

'So, what's the problem?'

'The problem is that you'd told me you were at home.'

She stares at me and says nothing. But I can see on her face that she wants to say something, she's desperate to shut me up, and instead she's forced to live with the sense of failure of someone who doesn't know what objection to raise. It's her job that's made her like that; I've never taught her to find reasons for everything, not least because I know that often there are no reasons and it's best to stay silent.

'It isn't so much because of the lie you told me. It's that I didn't think you could do it with an old man like that. If you'd come out of the front door with a smiling young man, I'd have headed off in the other direction, although I might have tailed you just in case. But not *him*. I need to know what you see in that old antique.'

At last a tear penetrates her armour. *I'm sorry, my darling, but to win a battle you have to be a villain. And, as you know, I'm an expert at that.*

'What do you want from me? Why do you go on ruining my life? Again and again and again!' she cries. Then she gets up, hurls her glass against the wall and leaves the room.

Left on my own, I look around. I don't like conference rooms: ascetic, perfect, frozen. Like meetings generally. I know I've gone too far. Perhaps I should go out there and apologize. Perhaps I should hug her. When did I last do that? I'd like to go back to the precise moment when I stopped putting my arms around her, the last time it happened. I'd like to tell that idiotic adult that Sveva will grow up and he will be old and filled with remorse.

Luckily, after a while, she reappears in the room and sits down. She looks calm, yet her smeary face betrays the fact that she has been weeping in solitude, perhaps in a bathroom as ascetic as the room where, right now, a father and a daughter have decided to talk to each other for the first time.

'You want to know what I see in that old antique, is that it?'

I nod. My mouth is dry.

'Well, daddy dearest, in that old ornament – which, just so that we understand each other, has a name and is called Enrico – I find everything I've always been looking for. What you and Diego have never been able to give me!'

There it is, I knew it. I've brought it on myself: I've given her too easy an out. I decide not to reply. The road to beatification is fraught with difficulties.

'In that man I have found affection, passion, understanding, refuge, strength, security. Since he's been in my life I have felt stronger and capable of facing up to everything and everyone. And I know that if I fall he will be the one who picks me up.'

'Finished?' I ask.

She doesn't look at me, but I know she would like to tell me to sod off again. But she doesn't reply.

My turn.

'OK. Refuge, I grant you. I admit that I wasn't one of those fathers who are prepared to sort out their children's lives, even if on the few occasions when I tried to do so I had all kinds of accusations thrown in my face. Passion, I grant you too. I know from personal experience that an old man still has a lot to give in that respect. And last of all, strength, I grant you. Yes, it's true that I've never been very strong, or at least that's what I like to think. But affection, understanding and security, no: I'm not letting you have those.'

'How can you be facetious at a time like this?'

'It comes naturally to me,' I reply with a smile. Unlike hugs, I can still dole out smiles without shilly-shallying. I give the odd one to Sveva, even though she barely gives me one back. I should be complaining too, but I realize it isn't the moment.

'Great, you always behave like an idiot. An old man of almost eighty who's still acting like a little boy. You're pathetic!'

'That's a big word!'

'You think you're beyond criticism, is that it?' she asks. 'You couldn't care less about what I'm telling you!'

If I had woken Federico when I got up from the sofa I wouldn't be in this situation – he'd be here now and would stop us accusing each other of failure. How I would like to be the child sleeping in the other room. In fact, if I could, I'd choose to be an orc, a monster with no purpose in life except to play, for ever and ever.

'No, I just think you like playing the part of the victim. I've made my mistakes. Your husband must have made his too, even though, knowing him as I do, I really don't know what he could have done that was so serious. But you can't say you haven't received affection and understanding. You've had affection – you just need to rummage around in your hatred a bit to find it. Understanding…well, you won't believe it, but you're getting some even now.'

She snorts down her nose. The conversation has left her shattered. Children make superhuman efforts to reveal a great truth to a parent, unaware that the parent knows everything already. And pretends not to see.

'You think you know everything about me, about Dante, even about Mum!' she says after a brief silence. She is still clutching her handkerchief, drenched with rage and frustration.

The salad on the plates is starting to rot, and soon the two waitresses will be coming back.

'I try to do my best.'

'And yet you know absolutely bugger all. You've never known anything at all, you know that? You know nothing about me, about Dante, who told me and Mum that he was homosexual over ten years ago. And you didn't know anything even about her either!'

My lips seem to be sticking together, and my heart is pounding. Caterina knew that our son was gay and never told me, even on her deathbed. I would have done so, at least before I breathed my last. I look at my arm and see that it's covered with gooseflesh. I don't know why, but I think something important is about to happen.

'What should I have known about your mother?' I ask in a thin voice, my fists clenched.

'Forget it…' she says, and gets up to leave.

I instinctively grip her wrist and stare her straight in the eyes.

She sits back down, her eyes fixed on her plate again.

'Mum had someone else. She was with him for five years!' she announces at last, in an icy voice.

If you get a punch in the face, the first thing you do is to touch it. It's an instinctive gesture. Your body is concerned to check that everything's all right, whether your jaw has been damaged, for example; whether you're missing a tooth. So my first reaction to Sveva's words is to bring my hands to my face and rub my jaw, as if someone actually had given me a thump. The sensation is the same. I feel groggy, and if there were some wine on that heavy glass table I'd glug it down straight from the bottle.

Noticing my silence, Sveva goes on. 'You're not saying anything?'

I haven't enough saliva to talk.

'Did you understand what I said?'

'Have you always known?' I manage to ask hoarsely, at last.

'Yes.'

'And you've never mentioned it to me…'

'Well, when it comes to that, I didn't tell Mum about your little adventures either!'

'Fine. They were exactly that: little adventures. But now we're talking about a five-year affair!'

'She didn't have the courage to leave you. She loved you —'

'Fuck off!' I shout, and leap to my feet.

Suddenly, for the first time in my life, I feel I actually hate my family. I hate Caterina, who duped me more effectively than I duped her, but particularly with Sveva. And Dante.

'Does Dante know too?'

'Mum never told him, but I think he worked it out eventually.'

'How long ago did it happen?'

'She left him just before she fell ill. One evening she told me she'd decided she wanted to spend her old age with you.'

'Great! So her lover got her best years, and I got her old age!'

'Don't you dare speak ill of Mum. At least she tried to love you for a whole lifetime! What was she supposed to do, spend her time with a man who didn't even look at her? And then, unlike you, she never had an old age. If you want to pick a fight with her, don't do it in front of me!'

I no longer know what to say. I feel confused and it's as if I can't breathe, so I head towards the door.

My grandson, perhaps woken by my daughter's rage, comes towards me holding that famous orc, the one I envy him so much. He looks at me, his face puffy with sleep, and raises his arms to be picked up. I hold him and give him a kiss. At that moment he seems like the only member of the family who isn't completely fake.

When I turn round, Sveva is sitting down again.

'Where is he now?' I ask harshly.

'He died last year.'

I feel the blood pulsating in my temples and a warm flush colouring my cheeks. I say goodbye to Federico, open the door and call the lift.

Sveva appears in the doorway with her son in her arms and her eyes glistening. As I wait for the cabin to come and save me, I instinctively bring my hands to my throat in a desperate attempt to get a bit of air. I've got to get out of here. I need to breathe, walk, think, forgive.

'How come I never noticed?'

'Dad, you couldn't even see her. We were invisible to you…'

We stare at each other for a long time, then, just before her tears turn into mine, I slip into the lift and press the button. By the time I've reached the street, I've understood one thing: if you get the seed wrong, you can't predict what crop you'll harvest.

Chapter Eighteen

The Second of Three Unattainable Women

We think life never ends and there's always something around the next corner that will change everything. It's a kind of deception that we practise on ourselves, so that we don't get too cross with ourselves for failures, lost opportunities, missed trains. For example, I spent forty years waiting to get close to Daria, a great flame of my youth that flickered alive after an evening talking politics in an old basement where we young people came together with the insalubrious notion of changing the world. The encounter didn't change the world, but it did change our lives. At the time I was a boy full of ideas and with great self-esteem (which, in truth, I've never lost with the passing years), thanks to which I managed to win the trust of Daria, a woman with a sound head on her shoulders and a slightly posh family behind her. She was more cultivated and more elegant than me, but she lacked a fundamental requirement that I had: confidence. She wrote stories and was about to finish a novel about a group of young people fighting to make Italy a better country. A kind of autobiography. It certainly wasn't an original idea, nor was it particularly well written, but I inspired her to believe in herself and finish the novel as soon as possible.

They say that only a real love has the power to change the course of people's lives. Mine, after meeting Daria, underwent remarkable changes. She was the one who persuaded me to accept the job with Volpe, which would later lead me to bump into Caterina. I have her to thank for everything that happened later. Or to blame, perhaps. Either way, Daria gave me a bit of her common sense, and I swapped it for my tireless optimism and enthusiasm, two qualities which, unlike self-esteem, I have squandered away in the course of my life. Of those months that we spent together, I still carry within me her loud, infectious laughter, her cold little fingers that were easily clutched, her mandarin-orange perfume that I found on my clothes in the evening. We were happy, and yet – I don't know why – we never kissed, perhaps convinced that we would be able to do it some time or other, or perhaps wishing to prolong the pleasure of waiting. In the end, we were savouring the best phase of a relationship, when you just have to touch the other person's skin to feel your heart beating.

To cut a long story short, Daria finished her novel and went in search of a publisher. I remember that after the first few refusals she told me she was going to give up, and for a few days I tried to persuade her not to give up, and not to be put off by difficulties. It's funny to think about it today, but I was just repeating to her what I said to myself in bed every night: not to stop wanting a different life, to go on pursuing her dreams, not to stop at the first setback, even if it seemed easier to do so. The difference between me and her, unfortunately, is that she alone fully believed my words, and she alone put them to the test.

And in the course of a few months she found a publisher willing to publish her novel. The funny thing was that by

the time it came out we were far away from one another. I
remember that I bought a copy and read it in a single night.
The next morning I was absolutely convinced that the book
was worthless. Like our story, incidentally. It went like this.
One night she stopped for a beer with her ex. I was only
ever a friend, and yet I couldn't conceal my disappointment,
even though I was, among other things, at the start of an era
in which being jealous and possessive was considered fascist
and backward-looking. The fact was that I noticed I was still
very backward-looking and I moved away from her, hoping
that Daria would come and get me. She didn't, unfortunately, and a fortnight later I was going out with someone
whose name I don't even remember, who smoked a lot and
drew comic books. Daria suffered from my sudden, incom-
prehensible detachment from her, and she didn't forgive
me, not even when, having left the horny-handed cartoonist
with the yellow fingers, I turned on my heels. At that point,
another of my conservative feelings, honour, forbade me
from pressing the point. I said goodbye to her and returned
to my life and my unflagging courtship of Caterina, even
though I couldn't sleep at night because Daria was so far
away. Over the next few months we hooked up several times,
but neither of us had the courage to make the crucial move,
until one day she got engaged to the one who would become
her husband.

There you have it. If I had suspected that day that the guy
with the Elvis quiff would be the last man in her life, I would
have set my conservative feelings aside and fought to hold
on to her. Instead I thought in my heart that sooner or later
the two of us would be together. I believed it for forty years.
Not even both our marriages, not even my children and hers,
ever distracted me from the basic idea: our bodies would not
be united, not even for a single night.

Every time I met her in the park, on the Metro, in a cinema, in a cafe, at the launch of one of her books, after three months or two years, I always greeted her affectionately and went away thinking that she would be mine in the end. Of course, if I claimed I stayed in love with her I would be lying. Love fades with time, like the colours in a photograph, but luckily you're left with the outlines that remind you of the moment that once was. For forty years I haven't loved Daria – I've loved the idea of being able to love her again. She gave me the opportunity to think that there's always an opportunity, that the things you wish for really happen, you just have to know how to wait.

Then one day seven years ago, her last book came out. I didn't even know about it when I bumped into her by chance in a pharmacy. Caterina had already fallen ill, and Daria hadn't been in my thoughts for years. She told me there was something about me in her novel. The next day I went to the bookshop and bought a copy. On the second page I found the dedication: *To Cesare, my unattainable love, for his courage, for his passion for life. With gratitude.*

I had to take refuge in the bookshop bathroom to hide my tears from the world, and I spent the night immersed in the novel, the story of two lovers who watch each other from a distance for the whole of their lives. In the end I put the book in the drawer of my desk and spent two hours staring at the blank screen of the television. It took me days to get back to normal life, given Caterina's illness and my last working days. In those pages I had found myself looking at a different Cesare, almost a stranger. Thanks to Daria, I had been able to see myself from a different perspective: hers. Books can do that too.

I absolutely needed to meet her. I promised myself I would write to her, then find her number and call her, invite her to dinner, send her a bouquet of flowers. But in that way I fell into the same error, thinking I had all my time ahead of me. Not even her big gesture of love gave me the necessary push to do what needed to be done. Forty years wasn't enough to work it out. By the time I did, it was too late.

I managed to get her phone number from a mutual friend, and for a month I held in my hands the little piece of paper with the anonymous figures written in biro. I didn't have the courage.

Then one morning I opened the paper and discovered that she had died of a stroke.

You spend your life believing that one day what you hope for will happen, but then you grasp that reality is much less romantic than you think. It's true that dreams sometimes turn up at your door, but only if you've taken the trouble to invite them. Otherwise you can be sure you'll be spending the evening on your own.

Chapter Nineteen

A Box Room Full of Memories

The phone has been ringing constantly for a minute. I'm lying on the sofa and I have no desire to get up to answer it. If Caterina were here with me she would do it, after snorting and cursing about my sly little smile. But she isn't here. I'm alone, really alone, perhaps for the first time in my life. I have to be sincere: I thought I was better at coping with the knocks of life. In old age you understand that few things are really worth getting worked up about: the betrayal and contempt of your family might be rightly listed among them.

For two days I've been stuck at home, a record for me. I'd like to go out, not least because I'm finding it hard to breathe. I don't know how Marino watches the days go by on his own from the perspective of his sitting room. And yet there's something holding me back, a little voice that's kept me company since I finished that sublime chat with my daughter and keeps repeating Sveva's last delicate phrase: 'We were invisible to you.'

I shouldn't have run away. I should have spent the whole day there with her, in that horrible conference room, and the night too, if necessary, perhaps lying on the carpet with some sheets of A4 as a blanket. I should have made her explain everything, every tiny detail of the story of Caterina and the life she hid from me. I would have been able, once and for all, to listen to everything that Sveva had to say to me. But seventy-seven years are too many to change – if I'd really wanted to I certainly wouldn't have waited for the most interesting part of my life.

When I left my daughter's office I was furious. I felt humiliated and betrayed, and I tried to build my days around that rage, the last slap in the face. But eventually it too – my rage – turned its back on me, weary of spending time with an old man shuffling from the sofa to the kitchen, and it flew away as soon as I opened the window. So I've been left on my own, without even that manipulative cat to keep me company.

You think you don't need anyone until you notice, one day, that you don't have anyone any more. And when it happens it's a right mess. I have my children, but it's as if I didn't. It isn't their fault, and it isn't Caterina's. Feeling jealous about someone who's no longer alive is idiotic, and yet that's how it is. Curiously, my wife is better able to capture my attention now that she's dead than when she was alive. I remember that one evening in bed she asked me, 'What would you do if I died?' I was too gripped by the book I was reading to get involved in a semi-serious discussion about our crisis that had been going on for ages. So I said, 'I'd sleep without earplugs.' She snored – loudly. When you're young you think that snoring is the prerogative of grannies and grandpas, that your wife will sleep angelically for ever among scented rose petals. Then you notice that at a certain age she starts turning into a pig, and it's at that precise moment that you understand that your youth has fled for ever. Anyway, she turned over and turned out the light. It was the only time we spoke about our crisis. Or rather, that she spoke. Or rather, that she tried.

I get up and go to the box room, a little room three feet square full of stuff that's no longer of any use to anyone. Storerooms are hostile places filled with a strange melancholy. Objects that have been set aside are nothing but memories that have been set aside, to be kept, but not always right in front of you. So, one afternoon when you push open the door of the box room, as you have done so many times before, you almost feel as if all those memories are cascading down on your head, your grief is so great.

I open a box and start rummaging around among the old photographs: travels, marriages, degrees, birthday parties, dinners, New Year parties and Christmases. If only there were a picture of one particular day in there. Nothing. And yet all I remember is getting up, shaving, getting dressed, making breakfast, then taking Sveva to school, and after a day's work, coming home, kissing my wife, having dinner, putting my children to bed and slumping on the sofa with Caterina. Nothing remains of all those parties but bleached photographs. In one of them Sveva is laughing, missing a tooth. I'm smiling too, and in the silence of the house my wail seems to echo like the sound of the photographs rustling in my hands.

Caterina was really beautiful, and always cheerful. And yet with the passing years her smile fades from the photographs, replaced first by a severe expression, then a sad one of infinite resignation. Caterina would have aged badly, I believe. If adulthood had stolen her smile, old age would have taken even the light from her eyes. Where I'm concerned, however, I feel that the inexorable passing of time hasn't managed to leave any marks. It's because I have a thick hide, while my wife was soft and welcoming, a little like Marino's armchair, which preserves his outline. Caterina took life's knocks and let them mould her.

I bring my trembling hand to my face in an attempt to explore a faded photograph from many years ago for something I didn't find back then: whether she was happy with her secret life, as stupid and in love as only a little girl can be. If she thought that he was better than me. But the photograph can't teach me all those things, so I drop it on the floor and look around. Long blonde hair spills from a box; I take it in my hand and pull out a Barbie, Sveva's favourite doll. It's still here in my box room, not hers. As they get old, the toys that children loved are loved in turn by their parents. I find nothing of Dante, however, perhaps because I don't know what his favourite toys were. I don't know anything about my son, beyond the fact that he likes men. He has never told me anything.

'What a great actress you were,' I find my lips saying. 'If you weren't happy with me, you just had to say!'

But I didn't listen.

'I know, but you should have pressed the point, taken me by the arm, hit me, thrown your soup bowl on the ground! You should have grabbed my attention!'

No one answers. But perhaps, if objects could talk, they would accuse me of dishonesty.

'Why the hell didn't you ever whack me one?' I yell at the room. 'Why didn't you scratch me? Why didn't you scream your head off at me? Why?'

Tears run down my face and slip into my wide-open mouth, but the taste of salt on my tongue doesn't make the moment any less bitter.

'It isn't right,' I continue. 'You didn't even give me the satisfaction of screaming my rage into your face! You should have told me. Even if it was right at the end, you should have told me!'

No, she didn't owe me anything. I never revealed anything to her.

'You could have stood up to me, and yet you learned to avoid me,' I whisper. 'And you taught our children to do the same…'

The phone rings again.

I wipe my nose and go to answer it.

It's Dante. I don't want to talk, but I try to make it sound as if I haven't been crying.

'Hello?'

'Dad, what's happened to you?'

'What's happened to me?'

'I've been calling you for two hours. I thought you might have fallen ill.'

My son has a slight tendency to overdramatize things.

'What are you talking about? I was just tidying the box room.'

'If you want to go on living on your own, you've got to bring the phone with you or you're going to give us a stroke.'

'Don't worry, I don't think Sveva gets worked up about that kind of problem.'

'Why are you saying that?'

His voice is penetrating – so much so that I'm forced to hold the receiver away from my ear. Even on the phone he sounds to me like one of those hairdressers who would rather be sitting in the customer's seat.

'Nothing. We had a bit of a tiff.'

'Another one? Will you two stop squabbling once and for all? You're always fighting, and you're always together.'

'Yes, but this time our squabble left a few more marks than usual.'

'Oh, come on. Anyway, I called you to invite you to dinner on Saturday. I want to introduce you to someone very special to me. I might even tell Sveva, so that you two can make peace and stop acting like children.'

'An important person?'

'Yes, but don't ask any questions. I'll explain everything tomorrow.'

Damn, Dante has decided to come out. Maybe he wants to introduce me to his partner? I don't know whether to hope it's the painter or someone else. Anyway, I've always hoped he would summon the strength to tell me the truth and, now that he's about to do it, I realize I'm not ready.

'Have you got a cold?' he asks.

'No, why?'

'Your voice sounds strange.'

'It must be interference on the line…'

'Fine. See you on Saturday.'

I put the phone down and go back to the box room, pick up the photographs from the floor and put them back in the box. Then I pick up the Barbie, just as there's a knock at the door. For two days I haven't seen so much as a bluebottle, and all of a sudden it seems as if everyone's just remembered I exist.

I go to the door and find Emma there, smiling and waving a plastic bag under my nose.

'Hi, Cesare,' she begins. 'I've just picked up a spit-roast chicken with potatoes and a bottle of wine. Can I come in?'

If it was just her and not the wine as well, I might have come up with some excuse – it isn't the best possible evening to support someone with more problems than me. But I realize I'm hungry, and the smell of the chicken inclines me to show hospitality to my neighbour.

I stand aside and let her in. She doesn't need to be asked twice and hurries into the corridor, leaving a pleasant smell of food behind her. And that's what I'm following when I emerge into the kitchen and find Emma unwrapping the chicken.

'It's like a morgue in here!' she says without looking at me. 'Why don't you turn the light on?'

She seems to be in a good mood. Last time I was the one who tried to cheer her up; this time it might be the other way around.

No sooner have I accomplished the task assigned to me than Emma asks me another question: 'What are you doing with a Barbie?'

It's only then that I glance at my hand and realize I'm still holding the doll.

'It was my daughter's favourite,' I reply, and put the toy on the dresser beside me.

'And you've kept it! What a lovely gesture!'

I should tell the truth: that it was Caterina who kept the Barbie. I'm not the kind of person to treat objects with affection – I've got enough trouble with human beings. But I don't say a word, partly because now that I can I want to seem like an affectionate father, and partly because, in fact, while I'm admiring the little platinum-blonde beanpole I seem almost to be feeling a bit of affection for her.

'What have you been doing? Have you been crying?' Emma says, interrupting my thoughts.

You can't hide anything from this blessed girl; in some respects she's worse than Sveva. She should be a lawyer; I could put in a word with my daughter.

'Nonsense. I've got a cold, that's all!'

She stares at me for a moment and then her face breaks into an infectious smile, so that I'm forced to turn round and get two glasses from the cupboard so I don't give myself away.

'I still haven't thanked you for the tablecloth,' I say. 'What a kind thought.'

'Don't mention it,' she says. 'I should be thanking you.'

I turn round and meet her serious gaze.

'I know it wasn't easy for you in the hospital the other day, but thank you for respecting my decision.'

It's strange to hear someone thanking me – I'm not much used to it. If people tell you over and over again that you're a good-for-nothing, in the end you convince yourself that you can't be anything but a good-for-nothing.

'Your cheekbone isn't swollen!' I say with satisfaction.

'Yes, luckily.' She winks.

'And how's your arm?'

'Better,' she says, and lifts her elbow to show me the bandages. 'I can move it now.'

Today Emma looks even more beautiful than usual, perhaps because she's wearing a cheerful expression that's new to me. Very few people have the gift of displaying joy, despair, rage, suffering, pleasure or enjoyment on their faces; with the rest of them you just have to make do with the mask that's visible to us. Perhaps Emma has decided to trust this lonely, crabby, old man and show him that pinch of joy that still shines in her eyes every now and again.

So I smile contentedly, and lay the table while she carves the chicken. The kitchen is filled with the smell of potatoes and meat, and I suddenly realize that over the past forty-eight hours I haven't consumed a thing apart from a little packet of cheese, an orange, a pack of crackers and a bottle of wine. Not quite enough for my dilapidated organism.

'He's not there?' I ask suddenly.

She becomes serious. 'No, luckily.'

I try to do my best: I carefully finish laying the table and pass her the plates.

When we're sitting down we're like a father and daughter having a normal dinner, rather than two disconnected souls trying to face a raging tide as best they can.

I don't know why, but I talk to her about Caterina.

'My wife had a lover.'

She looks up from her plate.

'I only found out recently. My daughter told me,' I add.

'Had you never noticed?'

'No. Or maybe I did and I pretended not to see.'

I don't know what has happened between us, for what obscure reason I feel like relating my private affairs to a woman I barely know. Just as I don't understand why she enjoys spending time with me.

'On the surface you struck me as a more contented man,' she observes.

Certainly, the interesting things about a person are all on the outside; inside all you find are guts, blood and regret. Nothing very attractive.

'I am content. Or at least I try my best to be so every day.'

She smiles. 'Good for you. To me you seem to be doing the exact opposite.'

I'm busy stripping the flesh from a chicken wing when Beelzebub makes his entrance, slipping through his usual half-open window.

'Oh, look who's here. It's the moocher!' I exclaim as soon as I see his nose appearing through the kitchen door.

He'd disappeared for two days, intent on some trail or other that he needed to pursue, and now that there's a chicken to chew on he shows up again. Emma holds out a piece; he stretches his neck to grab it and swallows it down in a second. After which he rubs himself vigorously against

the legs of his new heart-throb. He doesn't come anywhere
near me – he knows he's at fault and he doesn't want to try
and take advantage of the situation.

'I've decided to run away,' Emma says at last.

'Then it's true: you're not actually doing everything in
your power to be unhappy! And where will you go?'

'Away from here, perhaps somewhere up north, to stay
with an old friend. A long way from here, anyway.'

'And the baby?'

'By the time he finds out, I'll be miles away.'

I drain a glass of wine in one gulp. I think *life* must be a
woman: when it needs to point out a mistake you've made,
it doesn't beat around the bush. The fact that my wife
lied to me for so long and that Sveva still bears a grudge
against me now seem as nothing compared to Emma's
insurmountable problem. You have to learn quickly how to
observe other people's lives to keep from vomiting unfairly
on your own.

If there wasn't a child in the picture, everything would be
much simpler. But as things stand, he isn't going to accept a
separation.

I decide to say what I think: 'If you really want to break
free from him, you should seriously consider the possibility
of an abortion.'

She stares at me and I hold her gaze. *I'm sorry, Emma. The
old scoundrel in front of you has decided not just to smile enigmatically
and turn away.*

'If his child is involved, he'll never leave you in peace,' I
add.

She lowers her head. I brace myself for a scolding, or for
Emma to get up and leave, but she does nothing of the sort.
She picks up Beelzebub by the collar and puts him on her
lap.

'You're right,' she says, stroking his neck. 'That would be the right thing to do.'

'No, not right. I'd call it common sense. You'll only really be able to get away from him by giving up the baby.'

Beelzebub starts purring and grabs my attention. For some time now, I've found myself envying the most ridiculous creatures, like toy monsters and cats – anything at all that has absolutely no responsibility.

'I know. But I'm not about to destroy the only good thing in my life!'

'You're right, but I still had to say it.'

Try and sift through other people's lives – flick through their unacted desires, their regrets, their shortcomings, their mistakes. There's one thing you'll never find: children.

'I'd like to meet your family,' she says.

She can jump from one subject to another in a flash.

'They don't come here,' I reply straight away.

'Why not?'

'Well, this was their mother's house – too many memories.'

'And what about you?'

'I know what to do with memories – you just need to lock them away in the box room.'

Emma laughs, and her beauty blows me away once again as I wonder why she has chosen to spend her time in an old man's bare kitchen rather than out there in the world. But I know it's because sadly there are those who think they own other people.

'You're too beautiful to spend the rest of your life with a character like that,' I say suddenly.

She turns serious and blushes before answering, 'He thinks I'm part of his property. And he's so sure of it that he's persuaded me of it too.'

I shake my head. 'No one belongs to anyone, Emma.'

'Yes, I know that now.'

Beelzebub slips furtively away and goes into the sitting room. Perhaps he'll go back to his cat lady now that he's had what he wanted.

Emma gets up and says, 'I've got to ask you a favour.'

'Fire away.'

She picks up her bag and opens the clasp. 'But you've got to promise me that you won't think I'm insane. I know it's illogical, but when I saw them I just had to have them.' And she takes out two baby-sized romper suits, one pink, the other blue. She shows them to me smugly with a smile on her lips.

I can't help smiling too and I'm about to reply, but she holds up a hand.

'No, please don't say anything. Can you keep them for me? I wouldn't know where to hide them. You can give them to me when the time is right.'

If Marino were here with me, he would launch off on an endless whine about how I'm getting too heavily involved, that at the end of the day there's nothing I can do for her and that my behaviour is also getting a little risky. But I've never listened to Marino in my life, so why would I start now?

I nod and take the baby clothes. I need to make a swift calculation, but I don't think I've touched anything like this in almost half a century. When Federico needed to be changed or put to sleep with a lullaby, it was always time for me to disappear.

'OK, I'll keep them for you,' I say, and lay the little romper suits on the back of the chair next to me.

'Thank you,' she says, pleased, and holds out her hand, expecting me to take it.

But I stay where I am, wavering like a man standing on the shore before diving into the water. *Dear Emma, if I found*

it easy to respond to an affectionate gesture, I wouldn't find myself with
a daughter who hates me and a son who's scared of me. Most of all,
I wouldn't have discovered that my wife had another life. But that's all
too hard to explain.

Luckily her stubbornness outweighs my weakness. She
takes a step towards me and hugs me. If I had just returned
her gesture, she would have left me with a simple handshake,
but now I get to embrace this blessed girl who, of all the
places she could have found to live, chose the flat right next
to mine. They must teach people to hug as children – it all
gets fearfully complicated later on.

When we draw apart, Emma seems pleased, but I find that
I am drenched in sweat.

Seriously, at my age, should I really add another individual
to the wretched list of people I'm interested in? I've always
tried to keep the list under control, so that it didn't grow
beyond all measure. The more people you love, the less pain
you avoid. That's another reason I've never had a dog: I'm
sure it would immediately leap to the top position.

'I should really be getting back,' she says.

I watch after her as she walks down the corridor.

After she's gone, silence keeps me company again and the
flat seems even emptier than it did before.

I pick up the rompers from the chair and walk towards the
still-open box room.

'If you look after all these memories, you can also look
after the dream of a girl who has no room for dreams!' I say
to myself, and put the clothes in an old box.

Then I shut the door and go to phone Rossana.

Chapter Twenty

A Little Bell Ringing beside Your Ear

There has never been one single way of confronting things. I, for example, decided to turn up at my son's house with Rossana. Dante gives me a surprise, so I'll give him one. She said she was available, and it couldn't have been otherwise: the other day I revealed to her that there was a good chance of her son getting his job back. In fact, I can't claim too much of the credit: I went to see Sveva and explained the problem to her as if nothing had happened between us. She went along with it and listened to me as she would have listened to an ordinary client, then concluded with these exact words: 'Don't you worry. That criminal will cough up the very last cent!'

In short, I used Rossana as an excuse to get close to my daughter again. I needed something to let me turn up at her house without being forced to go over the things we talked about all over again. I was right: Sveva got so excited about it all that she even forgot to ask me anything more about Rossana. In any case, she'll find out this evening.

'Nervous?' my companion asks as we prepare to press the buzzer.

'A bit,' I say, and leave it at that.

In fact, I'm very tense, and not because in all likelihood my son is going to tell me something tonight that the rest of the family has known about for thirty years, but because I'll have to pretend to be something I'm not: an affable, sympathetic chap. Sympathy is overvalued anyway, and sometimes serves to cover up loads of rotten things, but that's how the world goes, and if you've gone to all the trouble of having two children you soon learn to mask boredom, pain and depression when they're around. Unless you want to make them unhappy too.

Dante has bought a place in Chiaia, in a little square at the end of a narrow, twisting alleyway, an elegant apartment in an old building with thick walls which, unlike some I could mention, protect you from your neighbours. Unfortunately, however, the flat is on the fourth floor and there's no lift. A lot of these little buildings, in fact, have no room for elevators. So I have to climb the stairs and sweat proverbial buckets just to hear my son tell me to my face that he's gay.

He's waiting for us on the landing with a big smile on his face. I wonder who he got all this excessive bonhomie from, whether I haven't transferred all the supplies in my possession to him, but a moment later he has already introduced himself very warmly to Rossana, even though it's the first time he's seen me with a woman by my side since Caterina left us. Neither, of course, has Sveva. I thought for a long time before taking this step, but recently I haven't cared much what other people thought. I mustn't allow the world to ruin the last days of my holiday.

So here we are, in my son's flat, which strikes me as just as strange as he is, in a tastefully furnished sitting room in which everything is in the right place – there's even a sofa at dachshund height, on which I have made the mistake of sitting down. I'm going to need some sort of crane to get myself back up again. That in itself demonstrates that there isn't much of me in Dante. I've never owned a house in which the objects were neatly arranged in the right place; I don't think I've ever even had a tastefully furnished sitting room. I've always delegated to other people – so much so that it was my wife who decided what I liked.

There's some jazz coming out of the stereo, and the air is perfumed with incense, and if there were a little stream running through the middle of the house I wouldn't be surprised in the slightest. There are paintings, prints, digital art on the walls, as well as sculptures and installations. One of these is right in the middle of the room: aluminium threads running from the ceiling to the floor. Each one holds a little manikin made of papier mâché. I lose myself in the tangle of metal wires until my son takes me by the arm and leads me to the kitchen, occupied by the scent of ginger and almonds and the presence of Sveva and Leo Perotti, the sociable artist who welcomes me as if we were two great friends meeting up again after years apart.

Rossana is smiling and open; she shakes hands, looks around, enchanted, and seems to be enjoying herself. 'It's lovely, this house is. It's like a hotel!' she says excitedly.

I turn around covertly and notice Sveva, leaning against the fridge with her hands clasped in front of her, darting rather surprised glances at my companion.

I look away and concentrate on Perotti revealing what we're having for dinner, which couldn't be more different from what I anticipated: farro risotto with saffron and carrots, sardines in tempura, pea and anchovy tart with red salmon caviar. I look around for a normal slice of bread, but the closest thing I can see is some rice crackers. Luckily there's a bottle of red wine on the table. I just fill the bottom of my glass to avoid a scolding, and meanwhile I glance furtively at Rossana, who doesn't seem to have noticed Sveva's rather ugly scowl, and is listening attentively to the gay artist as he explains the more recondite secrets of his dishes.

Dante comes over and whispers in my ear, 'Your Rossana seems nice.'

'Yes' is all I say, before the valiant Leo draws me into a conversation about macrobiotic cooking and the Mediterranean diet, two topics not especially close to my heart. In fact, everything concerning health and well-being leaves me cold, so while Perotti expatiates I find myself yawning loudly. I've forgotten my manners, the polite smiles and pointless discussions. I've been marked by years spent among the world's rejects; I know how to talk to a prostitute, but I don't know how to hold a conversation with a brilliant man. Sometimes I think that if you're born one way, you can't die another way. You spend a lifetime deluding yourself that you've changed direction, and at the end you discover that the shortcut led you straight back to the path you were already on before.

Luckily Rossana intervenes in the discussion with all her feminine energy, and I'm able to slip away inconspicuously. I go out on to the balcony and stand and watch the streets below. In Naples, in fact, your sense of hearing is of more use to you than your eyesight: it's a city that reveals itself through sound. In the alleys of Chiaia, for example, on summer evenings you can hear women's heels stepping confidently on the cobblestones, laughter in the distance or two glasses clinking just beyond the alleyway. Posillipo, on the other hand, seems mute, with its wide, deserted boulevards spreading silently over the hill, while the city just below seems wrapped in cotton wool. You need to know how to listen carefully to the nuances of the posh districts if you want to get to know them. In the old city, on the other hand, you need to be able to distinguish things; you need to pay attention only to the things that interest you, to separate out the sounds, like mixing recorded tracks on a piece of music. That way you can enjoy the clamour of the students wandering among the ancient alleyways, the rattle of cutlery from the trattorias, the bells that ring out on Sunday morning, the calls of the street vendors, the hoarse, unsteady voice of an old man playing the accordion at the foot of a battered and forgotten basilica. But to enjoy all of that, you have to cancel out the buzz of the mopeds that infest the streets, the shouts of women getting worked up about nothing, the voice of a Neapolitan singer bursting from a car window.

'Come here. I've got something for you,' Perotti says as he appears on the balcony and takes my arm.

I'm about to claim my limb back when, once again, I notice Sveva standing beside the fridge, scrutinizing me severely. She's been keeping her eye on me and Rossana since I came in. I don't think she's too impressed with my companion, but to be honest I didn't expect anything else. Sveva is too angry with life to enjoy its many facets. As far as she's concerned, everything is black and white, and she could never socialize with someone who doesn't share her social background.

Luckily my old artist friend steals me away from such thoughts and drags me into the sitting room. I'm leaving Rossana at the mercy of my two children, which isn't really a very nice situation for her to be in. But she'll know where to find me – if she can hold an old opportunist like me at bay, she can deal with a shark like Sveva.

'I thought you liked it the other evening,' the artist says, pointing to the picture of Superman that's resting against the wall, 'so I thought I'd give it to you as a present.'

I look first at the painting, then at him. Superman and Leo Perotti have the same conceited expression on their faces. It seems too much. 'Now, I can see that you're keen to make an impression, but this really seems too much!'

His smile vanishes as if by magic, and only the superhero goes on enjoying the scene with an amused smile.

'Because, look, you don't need my permission, and you don't need to be nice whatever the cost. Dante is an adult, and luckily his choices don't depend on me.'

'I was just trying to be nice,' he says, a little less affable now than he was two seconds ago, 'and not because I'm interested in having your permission, but because I love Dante and I like to see him happy.'

Perhaps I've been underestimating the painter. Now that I've insulted his dignity, he seems a bit tougher.

'And he's happy if you and I agree. Is that right?'

Now he looks at me with a hint of superiority. 'No. Dante would be happy if you really accepted his way of life.'

'And who says I don't?'

'Well, if he's never talked to you about me until today, there must be a reason.'

I'm starting to develop a soft spot for good old Perotti.

'If he's never talked to me it's because he didn't feel like it. I've always respected his will. I've never forced him to tell me anything.'

'But you've never encouraged him either,' he replies stoutly. 'Maybe that's all Dante needed…'

Just see if I'm going to let my son's partner treat me like an idiot at my age. Among the many accusations over the past few days, the last one I needed was that I'd never encouraged Dante to tell me about his sexual tastes. I'm about to reply in my own way, but Sveva comes into the sitting room holding a dish. Damn it all, from the frying pan into the fire! I half close my eyes and for a minute I think I'm about to apologize to Perotti, not because I think I've made a mistake but to escape Sveva's look of rancour behind my back. So I take a step forward to move away, but she grabs my arm. Everyone seems to want a part of my arm this evening. I turn around, smiling, but Sveva isn't smiling at all. In fact, she looks worried.

'What is it?' I ask.

She takes the glass of wine from my hand and begins impetuously. 'If you hadn't spoken your mind about Enrico the other day,' she says under her breath, 'I wouldn't say anything about this Rossana that you're consorting with.'

A slightly shrill laugh from my friend emerges from the kitchen and reaches the sitting room.

Sveva half closes her eyes and frowns as if she had just heard someone scraping their fingernails down a blackboard.

I go on smiling.

'Where did you find her?' she asks.

'Why, don't you like her?' I say, increasingly amused.

'Well, let's just say she's a little bit exotic…'

'Yes, you're right. That's the right term, the one I've never managed to find. She's exotic, extravagant, colourful.'

She looks at me, perplexed, and says nothing.

'You see, daughter of mine, this old man that you see in front of you needs a bit of extravagance, a bit of colour to keep from suffocating. It would do you no harm either.'

'Why do you always have to act the clever clogs? Haven't you thought about us? About how humiliating it might be for your children to see you in the company of a woman like that?'

'What's wrong with her?' I ask, not smiling now.

She only lowers her eyes for a moment, then she answers

harshly, 'She's not right for you, not right for this family. And I think that her presence here is offensive to our mother's memory as well.'

At that point I explode and stifle a shout. 'Don't talk to me about offensive. What's offensive is that no one came to tell me that my son is gay. That's offensive! It's offensive that my wife had an affair with someone else for five years. And what you're doing to your husband is offensive too, if you want my opinion. We all offend someone else. You're not all that different from me.'

She goes on staring at me in silence, her eyes full of grievance and humiliation.

'Now, let me live what's left of my life in a bizarre way. I've spent a whole life surrounded by normality, and just smelling the stench of it turns my stomach.'

A moment later, the others come into the sitting room carrying plates, broad smiles on their faces. I look at them mutely and sit down at the head of the table. It has only taken my companion five minutes to be accepted by Dante and his partner, while during the same amount of time my daughter has come to despise me even more. It's strange, the more advanced I get in years, the quicker things tend to go for me; I'm like a marathon runner racing against himself, constantly trying to get better. By the time I'm on my deathbed people are going to hate me the second they look at me.

But Leo Perotti, rather than sitting as far away from me as possible, chooses the seat next to me. I give him a respectful look, because basically he's not a coward.

'Did you like your present?' Dante asks as soon as he sits down. 'Leo wasn't sure – he thought you wouldn't accept it. But I know you well: if you like something you're not going to turn it down!'

That's right. *You know me really well, my dear Dante – about as well as I know you.* Strange, and yet it seems to me that the only person at this table who really knows me is Rossana.

I smile again at Perotti, who smiles back, unconvinced. A shame, he's already given up the fight. So I dedicate myself to my regular adversary, the hardiest one of all.

'How come Diego isn't here? Another sudden work meeting?' I say, putting my napkin on my knees.

But Sveva doesn't even glance at me and instead serves Rossana, who immediately comes out with another of her comments: 'Mmm, this risotto looks delicious.'

Dante and Leo look at each other, amused.

I turn towards my daughter, waiting for yet another condemnatory look, but it doesn't come. Instead, she decides to surprise me and says kindly, 'It's farro. It's a bit like rice, but it isn't actually rice.'

I don't know if it was my tongue-lashing, but now Sveva looks calmer and more benevolent. Everyone seems calm, and determined to have a pleasant evening. Everyone but me.

'So, tell us,' Dante begins. 'How did you two meet?'

I knew it: my son is a dreadful old gossip who can't keep his nose out of other people's business.

'Rossana was a nurse of mine a few years ago,' I explain.

'Yes, of course. That's where we've met before,' my daughter says, and I can't work out whether there's a veiled intent behind her observation, and whether she somehow wants to ruin my dinner.

But it's Dante's evening – we're here for him – and I don't think she would do that to her brother. Nonetheless, I feel obliged to intervene to get my companion out of a sticky situation, so I decide to get straight to the point.

'So, what were you going to tell me that's so important?'

Dante looks at me, dumbfounded. Perhaps he thought I

would have been satisfied just to have worked it out, that the penny would have dropped once I'd seen his artist friend. *No, my dear Dante, for once in your life show a bit of courage and confront your old man, who is already quite nervous enough this evening.*

But he doesn't speak.

Sveva is the one who butts in, as always, and gets her brother out of his difficult spot. 'It's fine. I'll tell you later, in private.'

'No, let's do it a different way,' I say, and stare at Dante. 'Let me relieve you of the task. I'll speak!'

Then I take a long sip of wine and put my napkin on the table, ignoring yet another furious glare from my daughter.

Rossana kicks me under the table, but I'm already off.

'Dante, you're a homosexual! Everyone knows it. You've told everyone, even your mother. I was the only one who was left out, perhaps because you thought you would wait until I was dead. And yet I have two important pieces of information to give you this evening. The first is that I have no immediate plans to kick the bucket. The second is that I couldn't give a tinker's cuss about your sexual tastes. I love you and I will always love you, even if I've never said so, even if I've made so many mistakes with you and it may sometimes have seemed as if I didn't care about you at all. I admire you, as a man and as a son. I admire and love you and Sveva in the same way, you can be quite sure of it. There, that's what I had to tell you – to tell both of you –' I glance at my daughter too, 'and at last I've summoned up the courage. Now, if you like, we can go on stuffing ourselves with your food for the rest of the evening, or else I'll get up, take this lady by the arm and go.'

I lower my head and start eating, even though my trembling

hand doesn't allow me to hold my fork still. Sometimes it's a huge effort playing the part of the curmudgeon.

When I look up, I see that Dante's eyes are glistening, Sveva is wiping away a tear, Rossana is staring at her plate and Leo Perotti is staring at me.

I smile at him again, and he takes my hand and exclaims, 'You know, until a moment ago I thought you were a total bastard! You've changed my image of you in only two minutes!'

This Perotti fellow is a terrific chap.

I shake his hand and say, 'Well, if it comes to that, I've rethought my view of you as well. Now we're equals!'

Then we burst out laughing. Rossana joins in, and Sveva and Dante have no option but to play along as well.

The dinner continues at an even tenor, and even Perotti's macrobiotic cuisine seems good. I relax, not least thanks to the wine, and listen to the others telling stories and talking about themselves, something that seldom happens to me.

When I get up to go to the bathroom, Dante comes after me, turns on the light in the toilet and stands there staring at me.

'What is it? Do you want to help me take a crap?'

He smiles and replies, 'I wanted to thank you for your words. I know it must have been a great wrench for you!'

'You have nothing to thank me for – you're still in credit!'

'Don't be too hard on yourself. You weren't a bad father in the end.'

'That's not what Sveva thinks…'

'You know Sveva – she likes to complain and blame other people for the choices she's made.'

It's only now that I realize I've been wrong for the past few years. I should have been spending less time with my daughter and more with her brother.

'You're getting more and more like your mother,' I say
with a sigh.

He takes after Caterina; Sveva takes after me. It wouldn't
take a genius to work out which of us would have been the
better bet.

'Why didn't Caterina tell me at least?' I ask.

He seems calm and contented. 'Because I asked her not to.'

Simple. Too simple, even. If it's a choice between a son
and a husband, you protect the son. Always. If I go on living
much longer, God knows what truths I'm going to find out
about Caterina.

I close the door and sit down to pee. The bathroom is full
of strange creams and lotions, and the air smells slightly of
vanilla. Perhaps it's the candles; there are candles of all sizes
resting on every free space. How I envy people who take care
of the places they live in. Rossana is right, this place is like
a five-star hotel; I feel more as if I'm in a lobby than a loo.
Luckily one of the wiser decisions I've made over the past
few years is sitting down to pee, otherwise poor Perotti would
have had a heart attack at the sight of his lover's beautiful
toilet splashed with pee.

When I get back, I find Sveva sitting alone at the table
with her arms crossed over her chest, staring with great
concentration at her glass of wine. I think she's waiting
for me. Dante and his companion are in the kitchen with
Rossana. Incredible, but some kind of energetic alchemy
seems to have set in between them. I think it's time to leave
before my daughter starts spilling her unhappiness over me.

Instead she says, 'Sorry about before.'

'Forget it,' I say curtly.

Sveva looks at me for a few moments and says, 'I would
never have expected to hear you say something like that, and
in front of strangers too. You surprised me!'

'You're overestimating me.'

'Could be,' she says with a half-smile.

There are kitchen noises in the background.

I sit down beside her. With my elbow on the back of the chair next to me, I say, 'To come back to what we were saying, it seems to me that the choice of your Enrico is a bit weird too. That's why I haven't probed any further, because I worked out that you too are at that point in your life when you need a bit of extravagance. And perhaps you're just scared of taking a good hard look at the way you've changed.'

She lowers her head and says nothing.

Then I go on: 'I know fear is a nuisance – that insistent, irritating voice that keeps coming back the more you chase it away. And yet you know what I've worked out? That, in fact, that little voice is just doing its job. It's trying to save you from yourself. It's trying to warn you that if you don't move, pretty soon things inside you are going to start to rot.'

Sveva replies without looking up. 'The truth is that I feel confused. I don't know what decision to make…'

'You know the greatest extravagance of all?'

She shakes her head.

'Living by your instincts.'

My daughter gives me a puzzled look.

'Stop imposing pointless mental restrictions. If you follow your instincts you'll never make a mistake. Birds migrate every year without wondering why. So, we should do exactly the same: constantly move and not ask too many questions. I've asked myself *why* many times over the years and ended up stuck. Now I've got to recover. I want to migrate a little every day.'

'With Rossana?'

'Sure, why not?'

'So what should I do with Enrico? Should I migrate as well?'

'I *should* tell you to think very hard, but I don't feel like it.'

She sighs and nods her head, then comments at last: 'At least you're amusing me with your crazy theories.'

'Not bad for an old man…'

'Are you together?' she asks.

'She's just a friend, nothing more.'

'A shame. It might have been better.'

'In what sense?'

'Well, I'd be happier if I knew you had someone to look after you.'

My daughter worries about my health, about keeping me from drinking and smoking so that she can nag me for as long as possible.

'I can take care of myself, you know.'

'Yes, but you get worse if you're on your own too much.'

'You think I'm getting worse?'

'Well, if I'd asked myself that question before this evening, I'd have said yes.'

I snort with amusement. In the end, it isn't too difficult to hit it off with other people. You just have to get the words out, even if they don't want to come spilling out of their own accord.

At the door Leo shakes my hand as warmly as he did when I arrived. This time I return the compliment – after all, he's managed to hit it off with me, something not everyone can do, and then he loves my son, and maybe gives him the attention that I didn't give him. Dante hugs me. I let him do it, even though his sweet perfume makes me feel like throwing up. It's actually the gesture that's hard for me to deal with, but I prefer to think it's the perfume.

'I should go now,' I say.

I'm old, and old people don't feel strong emotions. They're already losing control of their bowels; if they started bawling as well it would be like spending your time with a baby.

Sveva comes down with us. 'Do you want a lift?'

'No, thanks. We'll find a taxi in the street, and it means we can have a bit of a stroll as well,' I tell her.

She gives Rossana a warm goodbye and a business card, then she hugs me, as her brother did a few minutes ago. So it's true that at a certain point in your life you make peace with your parents. I think it's what happens when brooding about your rage is more trouble than putting it behind you.

'Don't worry about us. We're happier than you think,' she whispers in my ear before pulling away.

I look at her carefully. She's always been elegant, like her mother, but this evening I find her beautiful as well, more sinuous. Perhaps even a bit less harsh.

'Kiss Federico from me,' is all I say.

On the way back, Rossana seems cheerful.

'That was a really lovely evening,' she says all of a sudden.

The crunch of dry leaves accompanies our conversation.

'Yes,' I say, wedging Perotti's painting under my arm.

In the end I couldn't say no. I'll hang it in the sitting room, so at least there'll be someone with a smile to keep me company during my sleepless nights.

'Your children are really lovely. And they're very fond of you.'

'Oh, sometimes I convince myself to the contrary, particularly where Sveva is concerned.'

'What are you on about? She's obviously in love with you, like all daughters.'

I pull an uncertain face, and she bursts out laughing and plants a big kiss on my lips. By way of reply, I lower my head and pretend to look at my watch so as not to let her see my red cheeks.

We walk along Via dei Mille in silence and dive into an ice-cream parlour that's still open, where, in defiance of Perotti's macrobiotic strudel, we buy two cones of apple-flavour ice cream. Then Rossana stops outside a darkened shop window, and I take advantage of this to look around and allow myself to be swept away by memories; the street corners are full of them, you just have to have a good eye and a vivid memory. There ahead of me, for example, there was once a bookshop with bright white walls and honey-coloured shelves. I used to stop every day and admire that blond wood which was held together as if by magic, without screws or nails, and made the shop look like a big sailing boat. Nowadays there are no shops as beautiful as that, at least not here in the city. At the time I was seeing a girl from the Umberto high school, just around the corner from here. In fact, 'seeing' doesn't really capture it – I was properly in love with her. I always fell in love with the girls I went out with. Falling in love and I got on just fine, but as for the next feeling, the one that people call actual love, we never quite clicked. But that's another story, and I was talking about the bookshop, where I took refuge one day when it was bucketing down and my girl couldn't bring herself to come out of school. I remained bewitched by that magical place, and by books in general, and began to think that one day I might have a bookshop all of my own as well. Instead something happened that altered my life, one of those little invisible crossroads that make you change direction. To cut a long story short, among my many youthful amorous adventures there was the baker's girl downstairs from where we lived. For her I swiftly abandoned the schoolgirl from Chiaia and the old bookshop. With the baker's girl, however, things didn't work out: she worked impossible hours and brought me hot panini every time we met. I imagined the future and saw myself enormously fat and bored, so I left her too and dedicated myself to my studies. Shortly after that came the coveted accountant's degree which made me walk along the path that has led me here. If only I hadn't met the baker's girl at that point, I might have married the schoolgirl and gone on visiting the old bookshop. Perhaps I would have been given a job at the shop and risen through the ranks there rather than at Partenope Services.

However, one day, when I already had Sveva, I was in that part of town and I noticed that my beloved bookshop wasn't there any more, and that it had been replaced by a women's shoe shop, yet another one. It was at that precise moment that I realized what I had lost, how life had deceived me with the curvy figure of a baker's girl. I don't know if I would have been any good as a bookseller, but I do know that sometimes in life you become aware of a little bell ringing beside your ear. It can happen when you're with a woman, or in a specific place, or when you're busy with something you like doing. There, if I had to give a piece of advice to my grandson Federico, just one piece of advice, it would be this. When you hear that little bell, look up, and look straight ahead – you have reached one of those invisible crossroads, and I assure you that it takes only a moment to make a terrible mistake.

Once I arrive home I pick up a hammer and two nails and go straight into the sitting room. It's late, but who cares? Just this once I can wake the neighbourhood.

I put Superman in the middle of the sitting room wall, just above the sofa, and look at it, enchanted.

'Yes, I like you!' I exclaim.

Just as I like Leo Perotti. I like Dante and Sveva, Rossana, Emma, Marino and the cat lady. Perhaps this evening the old fellow who's groping my daughter wouldn't seem so bad. The truth is that you can't always be grumpy and hateful, or people start believing you.

I go into the kitchen and pour myself a glass of wine. When I close the fridge door I see Beelzebub looking at me drowsily. I offer him my last slice of cheese, then pick him up by the scruff of the neck and carry him into the bedroom. Before undressing, I stroke his head and his purring makes me smile. Yes, it's as I thought: I really am getting too old.

Chapter Twenty-one

In Vino Veritas

The doorbell rings. I curse. It will be Signora Vitagliano wanting further information about Emma's life. It's the right time to tell her to get lost.

I press my iris to the spyhole and study the landing: the form of Marino occupies the whole of the visible space. I am startled – I don't know how many years it is since he's left his house. I open the door. He looks at me and smiles; I do the same. Then we stand there like that, incapable of hugging.

'You managed to extricate yourself from that filthy armchair!' I say euphorically.

'Yes,' he admits. 'There was something I wanted to tell you. I was about to pick up the phone, then I thought: *what the hell, go up there and tell him in person!*'

'I'm proud of you. Come on, let me offer you a glass of wine.'

'Thanks, Cesare, but you know I can't drink wine.'

I invite him to sit down and fill up a glass for him as if he hadn't said a word.

'Marino, how much longer do you think you have to live? I want to be frank: you haven't got long. People die when they're eighty. That's just how it is – there's nothing you can do. In fact, you've been lucky to get this far! So, if you have a glass of watery wine right now, who's going to tell you off?'

Marino gives me a sidelong glance and laughs.

'You are a card, Cesare,' he says and takes a long sip. Then he sets the glass down and looks around. 'Your kitchen isn't as I remembered it.'

'Meaning?'

'It was cleaner, tidier, more welcoming.'

'Of course it was! The last time you came Caterina was still here. It's the lack of her that makes you notice the absence of all those qualities.'

Marino laughs again.

I fill his glass again and invite him to raise a toast.

He looks at me as if I were mad.

'No, Cesare. You're trying to kill me today...' he says hesitantly.

'Yes, I'd like to see you popping your clogs after enjoying a good glass of wine, or between the thighs of a beautiful woman!'

'How have I managed to remain friends with you for so long?' he asks and drinks down his second glass.

'In fact, you've been very patient. And never like my children, who have been forced to spend time with me since the day they came into the world!'

'What a fine burden you placed on them,' he observes, and bursts out laughing, spilling wine on the floor and on his worn flannel trousers.

'You look like one of those old men who wet themselves!' I say, laughing too.

'Cesare, I *am* one of those old men who wet themselves!' Marino replies, pouring himself another drop of wine.

'Yes, you're right!'

I'm laughing and shaking so much that I can't bring the

glass to my lips. It might be the alcohol, it might be the joy of having an old friend back in my kitchen, but I can't help it, and I find myself helpless with laughter, like I often was in school as a little boy. Perhaps it's the fact that we're not supposed to laugh like that that makes us lose all restraint. Uncontrollable laughter is like weeping – we use tears to free up all that accumulated energy.

There was a time when Marino and I used to laugh a lot, before the old soul decided to withdraw from life. One day about forty years ago, a scowling, arrogant person came to the Volpe office. That person was me, taken on for a favour that Signor Volpe owed my brother. Caterina was there, as I've said. But not just her. There was another person too, an ordinary little chap with a pleasant smile.

'This is Marino, my brother-in-law. He'll explain how things work around here,' Signor Volpe said before disappearing and leaving me with this clot, staring at me beatifically.

Marino was forty at the most at that time, and yet he already struck me as old – so much so that I found myself staring at him and wondering how old he was.

Then he held out his hand and introduced himself.

I exchanged his soft grip and said, 'I'm Cesare, and I hate this job, so don't expect too much, because in a few months I'm going to be out of here!'

He stood there open-mouthed and a moment later he burst out laughing. I couldn't have known it at the time, but that laughter would bind us together for the rest of our lives. Marino soon became my most intimate confidant, the reliable friend who picked me up in the morning and walked me home again in the evening, who covered for me at work if I was busy with one of my extramarital adventures. He was like a child in the body of an old man; he was one of those people who have only half grown, their body heading straight for late middle age while their character was still anchored in the first years of life. Like a child, Marino was full of enthusiasm, generosity and life, but like a child he was also insecure, fragile and fearful. I was like a strict father to him, while he for me was the perfect friend, the kind that everyone should be lucky enough to meet sooner or later.

For a while our relationship was confined to working hours, and then one day, aware that after Dante was born we were looking for a new place to live, he came out with this: 'The flat above mine is for sale. It's a reasonable deal too. Why don't you and Caterina come and take a look?'

We found ourselves living above him, and met his wife Paola and his children Sebastiano and Antonia. Our lives were intermingled for years: dinners, parties, graduations, Christmases, card games, sometimes at ours, sometimes at theirs. Our shared life involved constantly going up and down the stairs, and my children fell asleep next to his with the television on. Every now and again we had a visit from the cat lady (although she wasn't yet a cat lady at the time), then married to a very sad man who loved television more than he loved her. Even though she had never had children she was full of enthusiasm, she always wore brightly coloured clothes, she smiled at life and often told us about the pupils she taught. She was a very resolute character, and a little out of the ordinary, a kind of overgrown flower girl. And yet her company made the evenings jollier.

And that was how the years passed, until the christening of Marino's grandson, Orazio, Antonia's firstborn. That evening I remember my friend was wearing a grey suit that made him look even more exhausted than usual.

During the ceremony he took me by the arm and whispered, 'Sebastiano is moving to London next month. They've made him an offer he can't refuse.'

I looked at him and smiled, but he didn't smile back.

'There are moments that mark your life for ever,' he went on, 'and one of those is when your children leave.'

'Well, it means you'll be able to start courting your wife again!' I said, joking.

But Marino wasn't in a joking mood. 'Paola is ill. She has Alzheimer's,' he said and gripped my arm.

I looked at him open-mouthed, but he went on talking as if nothing had happened. 'I'm happy for Sebastiano and also for Antonia. The young people need to think of their own lives.'

'Fine,' I said in a whisper. I would have liked to ask him something more, but he didn't let me.

'And yet you get used to them in the course of your life, don't you?' he said, as Antonia called him over for a photograph.

You don't get used to it – you try not to change things. That's different. That was what I would have liked to say to him, but he was already far away.

Then, the next year, that day came, the most terrible of all. He received a phone call from England early in the morning. Sebastiano had died in a car crash. Those were frightening months. Marino was a skeleton who only managed to keep walking by inertia, just because his wife needed him. He seemed to be getting old at twice the speed of everyone else, as if he lived in the body of a dog and one of his years equalled seven of ours. As for me, I tried to help him as best I could, at work and at home, but he didn't even seem to notice.

Four years later, Paola died too, and my friend found himself on his own in the big flat that had been filled for decades with laughter, shouting, tears and grumbling. Antonia tried to make him move in with her, not least because Marino had retired by then, but the stubborn old fellow wouldn't hear of it. But in the evening he ate at our house, watched a bit of television and then went back downstairs. I found myself feeling sorry for him, even though over time that pity turned into admiration. I didn't think he would get over all that had happened, but with the passing months he managed to stand his ground. Life has not been kind to him, and yet Marino has kept going. That was when I worked out that it's not that some people are braver than others, it's just that some people confront pain when it needs to be confronted.

But one day he called me and asked me to come and see him. I stepped into the silence of a house that I didn't recognize.

'I wanted to tell you that from now on I'm not coming to yours for dinner,' he announced with a smile.

I returned the smile, thinking that he needed to get his autonomy back.

'Tell me the truth. You've found some company that's better than ours,' I said with a wink.

He laughed the way he used to, but then he immediately grew serious again and replied, 'Cesare, I'm too old for these things. It's just that I'm tired of running away.'

I could have insisted, and perhaps if I'd only guessed that his house had become his tomb, I would have done. Instead I thought that basically he was right, and I went on joking, as we always did: 'There are some things you're never too old for, Marino. And in the meantime, they've invented these magic pills.'

He poured me some wine and didn't reply.

During those years, Eleonora Vitagliano's husband had moved on to a better world as well, and for some time I had found myself thinking that the two of them might have kept each other company. She had stopped teaching, she didn't go out much and she was starting to develop an unfortunate fixation with cats – to the extent that I often bumped into her on the landing with a cat she had just picked up in the street. There is more than one way to confront loneliness: some people lock themselves up at home; some become too fond of animals; and some learn to commune with silence.

'You haven't thought of taking up with Eleonora Vitagliano?' I asked Marino after a while.

'What are you on about?' He jumped up from his armchair. 'Have you gone mad?'

'Well, you're both widowed and alone, you've known each other for ever – why not keep each other company for a while?'

'Cesare, don't talk nonsense. And have you seen what she's like these days? She seems to have gone off her rocker. I can't even bring myself to invite her in for coffee – she stinks of cat food.'

I smiled.

He was right: desperation has its limits too.

So I said, 'Yes, I think you're right. Loneliness is better,' and held out my glass for a drop more wine.

We said goodbye when it was dinner time.

When I told Caterina the news that Marino wouldn't be coming to ours any more, she observed irritably, 'Shame, I'd got used to his silent company.'

'Don't worry,' I said as I went to the toilet. 'He'll be back in a few days, you'll see. He can't just bury himself away at home!'

Eight years have passed since that evening. Long enough for Marino to make friends with grief.

'I came up to give you this…' Marino sighs eventually.

'Me first,' I say.

He looks at me curiously. His cheeks are red and his breathing is heavy.

'The girl is expecting a baby. I wanted to tell you before…'

Marino sits with his glass half-way to his lips for a second, then leans back.

'Does she plan to keep it?'

'That's what she says.'

'I was right: we shouldn't have got involved. I'm old and fed up with hearing people's problems.'

'What was I supposed to do? I'm just helping an unfortunate woman.'

'You're getting too mixed up in the whole thing. The letter is one thing; having her sleep at yours is quite another.'

The laughter of a few minutes before is now a distant memory.

'And what if he somehow found out?' he goes on.

And blow me if old Marino doesn't start shaking like a jelly.

'Don't worry, I've already thought of something to take the wind out of his sails.'

'You're crazy, you know that? You're just a poor old man – you should pull yourself together and accept the fact sooner or later.'

'No, I've decided to accept bugger all. If old age claims to have won the day, it's still got a bit of work to do!'

Marino looks at me uncertainly as I fill his glass once again.

'So?' I ask. 'What did you want to tell me?'

He sets down the glass and stares at me, then, in a proud voice, he replies, 'I've brought you the letter. Orazio and I managed to print it!'

Something that would be an ordinary action for the world becomes a mountain peak to climb for us. The truth is that technology should have more respect for old people. I take the envelope and turn it round in my hands. Sometimes the wild gale of initial enthusiasm fades away to become a light spring breeze. I pick up the bottle again and pour out the last finger of wine left in it.

Marino doesn't complain: he's on my side now.

'To Emma's safety,' he says, then raises his glass and brings it close to mine.

He is so happy to be able to help a girl in difficulties that I can't bring myself to tell him that the letter drenched in the sweat of his efforts will end up in the bin a moment after he leaves.

'To her safety...' I say.

We clink glasses, then I walk him to the door. Perhaps I should walk him all the way home – he seems a bit tipsy. But then so am I, and I'm old too. But, unlike Marino, I'm doing everything I can to forget the fact.

I throw the letter in the kitchen bin and go back into the sitting room.

Until you experience pain in the first person, you can't understand it. And yet how many people use the words 'I understand you' incorrectly? 'You don't understand a bloody thing, my friend' – that's what we should really say. I was playing cops and robbers; Emma was facing reality.

I turn around. I lie down on the sofa and put my plaid blanket over my legs. Then I half close my eyes, in spite of the smell of mildew that seeps from the wool. In this house even the objects smell of old age. The tough thing is to get used to it.

Chapter Twenty-two

In My Own Way

I've just made myself comfortable when the doorbell rings again. My peace is over, and it's my own stupid fault. Now I can't even rest my gaunt buttocks on the sofa for a moment without someone coming to look for me.

This time it's Eleonora.

Clutching her stick, she looks me up and down and begins: 'The estate agent's coming up. You told me I could call you…'

I run my hand over my face and put on a jacket. When I come out on to the landing, the man selling flats is already in the doorway of the Vitagliano household. In his wake are a young couple looking around with a perplexed expression. I walk up behind them, trying my best to breathe through my mouth, until the estate agent becomes aware of my presence and suddenly turns around.

'He's a friend of mine,' the cat lady says.

The man holds out his hand, and I shake it, looking at him and his clients, who give me a chilly smile. I would like to explain that Eleonora really is only a friend and that I have nothing to do with the stench filling the scene, but I have more important things to do.

Meanwhile, as the couple walk from room to room with

Eleonora, I take my man by the arm and say, 'I need to talk to you.'

He studies me and replies, 'Tell me.'

'How are the viewings going? I mean, is anyone really interested in the flat?'

'Not for the moment, no, but it's a good area, the building is elegant. Someone will turn up to buy sooner or later – we just have to wait. Of course, if the lady would present the house in a better condition, everything would be easier,' he concludes, amused.

I'm not amused at all. 'That's exactly what I was trying to get at. I am a patient and understanding man – I know we all have to work – but the next time you're so bold as to tell the lady how to look after her apartment, I'll throw you out. You *and* your lovely clients.'

His sly smile vanishes from his face in an instant. 'I was saying it for her benefit. To ease the sale. I'm just doing my job.'

'There you are, good man. You do your job and don't give unwanted advice.'

He lowers his head.

'Because…You want to know the truth? The lady has no intention of selling.'

'I don't understand…'

'No, you do. You're not stupid. You know very well that the order to sell doesn't come from here. And you also know that for an old woman, seeing strangers coming into your home every day isn't exactly reassuring.'

'Listen, I don't know who you are. I'm just respecting my mandate…'

'Exactly, your mandate. That's exactly what I wanted to talk to you about. You've got to give up your mandate, and never bring anyone here ever again.'

This time the estate agent loses patience and puffs out his chest. 'My client is not you. It's Signora Vitagliano's niece. If anybody does, she would have to be the one to ask me to call off the sale.'

I sigh. I had hoped I wasn't going to have to do the quick-change thing, but the little chap was being unnecessarily stubborn. I look at him and smile, not least because he gives off a pleasant smell, and in circumstances like these, such details are of some consequence. He stands there motionless, waiting for my reaction, with his nice grey suit and his green tie, his little file full of useless sheets of paper and his hair full of gel.

Then, a moment before the young couple interrupt us, I reply, 'I don't believe we have understood one another. I am a retired general of the financial police. If you don't stop spewing people into this lady's house every day, I will find myself obliged to ask my former colleagues to pay you a visit at the first opportunity. I don't believe your employer would be terribly pleased with that.'

He turns bright red and doesn't reply, not least because, incredible though it might appear, his clients, in spite of the stench and the zigzag path they have to cut among the cats, seem to be keen on the property.

'We like it,' the young woman begins, and smiles at each of us in turn.

Eleonora anxiously opens her eyes wide, so I am forced to give her a reassuring wave, and a moment later I address the estate agent once again.

'Fine, we'll get out of your way,' he says and walks his clients outside.

But the girl doesn't seem to want to give up. 'Shouldn't we talk to the lady? We're interested in the flat,' she says once she's out on the landing.

But the agent stops her straight away: 'No, let's go to my office and I'll try to explain.'

'They really seemed interested this time,' Eleonora says once we are on our own.

'No, I had a word with the estate agent and he understood that he should stop bothering you, because you're not selling the flat.'

'What?'

'He knows not to come here again,' I say, 'because you're not selling.'

She looks at me, perplexed. 'What did you tell him?'

'What? Aren't you pleased? Isn't that what you wanted?'

Eleonora comes over to me, her hair ruffled and her mouth twisted into a strange grimace. 'I never asked you to tell the truth. I just didn't want the estate agent to make any more comments about the house. You were only supposed to stand beside me. And my niece is going to be furious!'

I half close my eyes and try to calm the fury that's starting to seethe in my veins. What an idiot I am for bending over backwards to help a woman who's confided in me about a problem she has. The fact is that I have my own way of resolving problems but – I don't know why – women don't always like it.

'Eleonora, listen,' I say. 'You told me to help you, to come to your aid, and then you change your mind. I don't have time to waste!'

'I just wanted you to tell him not to bother me at all hours.'

'Then you expressed yourself badly,' I say, and set off towards my own flat, while one of her cats, taking advantage of the moment of confusion, slips between my legs and hurtles downstairs.

'Cesare, don't be a stubborn old fool. Come here. We have to call the agency and explain the situation properly.'

I turn and stare at her in disbelief.

By way of reply, she lowers her head and adds, 'Come on, damn it. Help me to resolve the problem.'

'I've already helped you,' I say with infinite patience.

'What am I going to tell my niece?' she says, on the brink of tears.

It's the first time in forty years that I've seen her like this. She has always been an energetic woman who's used to speaking her mind and issuing orders, first to her husband and then to the cats. But the Eleonora in front of me now is an old woman who's still playing at being strong, even though she no longer is.

'The truth,' I say. 'Be honest. At our age lies are short-lived.'

Then I leave her in the doorway and close the door behind me.

Nearly eighty years I've had – still not enough for me to understand women.

Chapter Twenty-three

An Unstoppable Flow

'Open the door!'

It's one o'clock in the morning and the voice on the entry-phone is Sveva's. Puzzled, I stare at the receiver. What on earth can have happened? I hurry out to the landing and hear her movements a few floors down. She's just called the lift. I lean over the stairwell and see my grandson's little hand clutching the banisters. In spite of the countless hypotheses that have poured through my mind in a matter of seconds, I can't think of a single valid reason why my daughter should turn up at my house in the middle of the night.

Unless she's running away.

If at a certain age you come back to sleep at your parents' house, there are two possibilities: either they're not around any more, or you're in trouble. And since I don't yet consider myself deceased, I opt for the second hypothesis.

'Don't ask!' she says as she emerges from the lift.

I pause with the question mark still on the tip of my tongue. *No, my dear Sveva, that's too easy. You turn up at this time of night, with your dazed and sleepy son, and you still refuse to answer my questions?* But obviously I keep all that to myself. I kiss Federico and take the little suitcase that Sveva is carrying behind her and follow them into the flat.

She slips off her jacket and turns towards me. Now at last she's going to tell me what's happened.

'Where can we sleep?' she asks.

I study her before answering. Her eyes are swollen with tears, her hair dishevelled and her lips are trembling. She can't have had a great evening. I turn towards my grandson, who can hardly keep his eyes open, and I feel terribly sorry for him. In all likelihood he's been dragged out of bed, he's witnessed yet another row between his parents and now he finds himself at his old grandad's house, without his father, his little bedroom, his toys.

You and your husband can hurt each other as much as you like, but keep Federico out of it. Bring him up far away from your hatred, keep him far from your regrets, hide him from your loveless glances. And if you really can't do that, then split up. A child growing up without one of his parents may be an incomplete and insecure adult, but one who grows up surrounded by hatred and violence will never be able to love. And there is no greater wrong that a parent can do.

'You can have my room,' I say harshly.

'And what about you?'

'I sleep little and badly. I'll be fine on the sofa.'

She takes the little one by the hand and goes to my room. I carry her suitcase in and find her with Federico lying on the bed, nervously trying to take his shoes off. I walk over and, without saying a word, move her aside and take over the job. Sveva is still holding his pyjamas and she throws them on the bed, then takes something from the little bag at her feet and goes into the bathroom. My grandson and I are left alone. He's already asleep, and I wish I was too. I slip him under the covers, then go to the cupboard and take out an old pillow that hasn't encountered a human face for God knows how long and bring it to the sofa, on which I have already put a blanket. I lie down and turn out the light, even though I already know I'm not going to get a wink of sleep – I'm too agitated. After a few minutes Sveva comes out of the bathroom and takes refuge in the bedroom. I hear her opening drawers and whispering something to Federico before the squeaky bedsprings tell me that she too has finally gone to bed.

It's strange. My daughter is in there, the same woman whose nappies I changed, whose bottom I wiped and whose tears I dried, and yet I feel embarrassed, as if my privacy had been violated by a stranger. Intimacy is created not by bonds of blood, but by living together. Even a mother, with time and distance, becomes a bit more of a stranger.

'Are you asleep?'

I suddenly look up and notice that she's in the doorway. I can't make out her face in the dark, but I'm sure she is wearing the penitent expression she always had when she did something wrong as a little girl. I remember once that when she was climbing on the dresser she knocked over my sister-in-law's whole dinner service. Caterina started shouting at her, so Sveva ran to me with the same grimace on her face as I saw this evening. Every time her mother told her off she ran to me, knowing that she would be safe. I've never been good at playing the part of the strict parent – it didn't come naturally to me; after the first two sentences I would burst out laughing and Sveva would join in. Then Caterina would come along and accuse me of being irresponsible, convinced that I was going to ruin my children's lives by making them grow up without an authority figure. Well, I had an authoritarian father and I didn't grow up any better than Sveva and Dante.

'No, I'm awake,' I answer curtly.

I can't hide my rage against her eternal silences. Caterina was the same, capable of saying nothing for hours, days and weeks, waiting for the resentment to fade. At first I'd thought I would go mad at the idea of not being able to release the tension and having to go on living together, then I also learned to ignore her rages. I wouldn't say they were nonsense, but I think her developing illness fed on that repressed energy. Every day my wife swallowed down her rancour.

Sveva sits on the edge of the sofa and stares at me. Even from such a short distance away I can't read her eyes.

'I'm sorry,' she says. 'I know I turned up at your house without giving an explanation but the truth is that I'm scared of your judgement.'

The first thing that occurs to me is to stretch my hand out towards her face, as I haven't done for an eternity. Sveva flinches uneasily before offering me her cheek. And then a moment later my hand finds her tears, as used to happen when she was a child and I wiped her tears away with my thumb before they could roll down her face.

'I don't know when you last did that.'

'I'm not really touching you,' I reply. 'The nuclei of our atoms never meet – they couldn't. Nothing touches nothing.'

'What's that?'

'I don't know. I once heard it in a documentary, but I didn't really understand it.'

She smiles and says, 'You watch too many documentaries.'

'Maybe, but they're the only thing that still stirs my curiosity. And curiosity allows me to feed my outmoded vanity!'

Sveva smiles broadly and so do I.

Then we turn serious and silent again, until she says, 'Diego and I argued. I think he suspects something…'

I sigh. Suspicion is the last step in the destruction of a relationship; by the time it comes, much has already been lost.

'Don't you love him any more?'

'I don't know…'

'So, no.'

'You don't believe in middle ways, do you?'

'Middle ways mean not taking the right road, the one that takes you straight where you want and need to go. Human beings are masters at idling to keep from reaching the goal they're scared of.'

'You've been given to philosophizing lately,' she replies sarcastically.

'It's not about philosophy; it's more that old age helps you to accept some uncomfortable truths. If you don't love your husband any more, you should leave him. Not for you – for Federico. Otherwise he will spend his childhood witnessing your rows and your frustrations. I'm sorry, I've tried to keep out of it, but now I feel the need to have my say. Make your choice. Don't be like me and the rest of the world. You don't know how many couples have stayed together just because they didn't choose.'

She pulls away from me, puts her elbows on her thighs and brings her hands to her face. Then she begins to swing back and forth, as Caterina did when she felt she'd been rapped. I can't help giggling.

Sveva turns around and gives me a puzzled look.

'No, it's just that you look like your mother. She often used to rock from side to side like that.'

'I don't remember that.'

'Well, a mother usually conceals her problems from her children.'

My words wipe away the hint of cheerfulness that was beginning to appear on her face.

'You think I'm making a mistake with Federico. Is that right?' she asks.

'Yes,' I admit, 'but I also think that's normal and no one can do anything about it. I made mistakes with you; you will with him; he will make mistakes with his children.'

She seems to have calmed down a little, so we sit there in silence for a while, with our breath interweaving and alternating in the night, as happened many years ago.

Again, she is the first to speak: 'Why don't you come and sleep in there?'

'Where?'

'In the bed.'

'There's not much room.'

'Who cares?'

'I'm fine here. Don't worry about me.'

'It was me I was worried about.'

I look at her curiously.

She frowns and goes on, 'It's because sleeping in that bed makes me feel sad...'

Hmm, I hadn't thought about that. People always linger in the objects that have accompanied them through their lives. Sveva has found her mother under the covers.

'OK then, I'll come and help you get through your melancholy,' I reply. 'But I warn you: I move all the time and snore like a pig.'

She laughs as she helps me to stand up.

We slip under the sheets, with Federico sleeping in between us.

Sveva, before turning out the light, stares at me and whispers, 'Thanks, Dad.'

'My pleasure. And anyway, thanks for what?'

When the darkness takes hold of the room again, I'm left alone with my thoughts as I study the ceiling, dappled here and there with specks of light from the cracks in the shutters. And for the first time in I don't know how long, I feel a sense of profound well-being. I turn around and look at Federico, who is sleeping facing up with his mouth open. Sveva has turned to face the other way, but I can still hear her breathing. So it's quite natural for my thoughts to return to the days when she was in the middle of the bed and her mother was the one with her back to me. Forty years have passed and yet history seems to be repeating itself, like an unstoppable flow.

What we are vanishes with our bodies, while what we have been is preserved in our loved ones. In Sveva I think I still see a little of Caterina, just as I used sometimes to see my grandfather's face in my mother's face. Who knows, perhaps one day I too will rise to the surface again with a movement, an expression, a smile from my daughter? And who knows whose eyes will notice?

Chapter Twenty-four

Like Clouds

This morning I got up earlier than usual. I gently slipped out from under the covers and went to the kitchen. Sveva and Federico were still asleep, lucky them. I spent the whole night being careful not to move a muscle so as not to wake my grandson. After a while my shoulder froze and my arm went to sleep, and yet that wasn't the worst sensation running through my body. About two hours after I fell asleep, in fact, I felt, regular as clockwork, the urge to urinate, which after a further sixty minutes became an irresistible impulse. My bladder was begging me to help it and free myself of all the useless liquid I had accumulated during the day. And I had actually overdone the wine at dinner somewhat. It is worth explaining (to the bladder, I mean) that a carafe of wine has the miraculous gift of rendering bearable even a melancholy and solitary evening in front of a pointless variety show.

The fact was that I needed the bathroom. The problem was that to get there I needed to turn on the light, put on my glasses and my slippers and shuffle along the corridor. It was impossible to do all that without waking Sveva and Federico. So I stayed motionless for the remaining four hours, lying on one side, because with a bladder swollen like a hot-air balloon lying on your back requires a superhuman pain threshold.

In short, the night had not been one of the most restful, but the day started off even worse, if that were possible. Over breakfast Sveva told me she would be going home that evening. I smiled, although I'm sure she could read the disappointment in my face. Not so much because she was deciding, once again, not to choose, as because her brief and unexpected visit had made me happier than I could have imagined. You get used to solitude, and forget that the night is less frightening if there's someone breathing beside you. And yet the decision had been taken and there was nothing I could do about it, so I merely drank my coffee in silence until she asked me if I would very kindly take Federico to school. In the past her request would have made me frown, but this morning I'm surprised to find myself smiling with satisfaction.

Less than an hour later, I was standing outside the school with Federico. I stopped there and gazed at the sky, clear but for a few funny-looking clouds drifting wearily towards Vesuvius. It wasn't a day to be locked up in a classroom. So I turned towards my grandson and said, 'Do you know what we're going to do now?'

He shook his head.

'We're not going to go in. You'll go to school tomorrow. This morning you're staying with grandpa!'

Federico smiled and opened his eyes wide, allowing a crabby old sod like me to feel, at least once, like a better person.

'And what are we doing?' he asked.

Indeed, what could we do? Where would Sveva have taken him? Then it came to me in a flash: Edenlandia, the amusement park that has welcomed all the children in Naples.

'Come with me,' I said, and headed towards the bus stop.

And so, incredibly, one Tuesday morning, I suddenly found myself in a theme park that I hadn't visited for over thirty years. When Federico worked out where we were going he started shouting, and for the whole journey he couldn't stop kicking his legs. The body always betrays our emotions, whether it be rocking back and forth, prey to indecision and fear, or happiness and excitement. In fact, the latter is much harder to conceal.

Unfortunately the smile with which I entered the park along with Federico faded from my face as soon as we had passed through the gate. He began to run from one attraction to the next, filled with joy, and I had no option but to join in with his enthusiasm, in spite of the listless melancholy that was running through me. Yes, because I'm like a guitar string, at peace with myself until someone plucks me: from that moment onwards I begin to vibrate ad infinitum. The sight of the place had taken me back in time. And at my age it's very dangerous to walk backwards.

It was the early 1970s and boom time for Edenlandia. Sveva was very young, and Caterina and I decided to take her to see for the first time the big theme park that was the pride of Naples and the whole peninsula. Caterina was keen, and our daughter was beside herself; the only one who couldn't really feel the same enthusiasm was me. At least, until I met someone – I think her name was Debora – a girl of about twenty who was standing with two other friends by a shooting range that gave away dolls as prizes. Caterina and Sveva were stuck in the House of Mirrors, so I approached the three and began my not very discreet flirtation with them. Soon I managed to win the teddy bear that Debora craved and won her heart. She thanked me and walked away with her friends, giggling and fluttering her eyelashes. I spent the rest of the day thinking of Debora's smile rather than the one on the face of my daughter, who by now seemed to have been driven crazy by the spectacle that was going on all around her.

It could have been the perfect day. I could and should have felt at peace with life, with my wife giving me loving glances, my daughter laughing gaily and clutching my hand, my city wanting to give me a day that I could frame and put on the mantelpiece. But I had met Debora, with her intoxicating body, her slightly childish giggle, her sensual eyes. So I pretended to be as happy as my family, even if I wasn't happy – not so much because my young muse had gone away as because she, a girl like many others, had made me lose sight of the beauty of the day.

By the exit I bumped into her again and, seeing me holding Sveva's hand and with Caterina beside me, she gave me a sarcastic look, possibly with a hint of contempt.

I looked at the ground in shame and took refuge in a clumsy smile directed at my daughter.

Federico and I passed by the Jumbo roller coaster and the Old America Far West village on our way to the famous Chinese Dragon, a kind of train that has been running round in a circle for half a century so that old fools like me can catch a stupid tassel dangling in the air as we go by. Well, we went round three times just to try and grab that stupid tassel, and the third time Federico said he was getting bored and wanted to go and buy some popcorn, but I wouldn't listen to reason: we weren't leaving until I had attained my goal. I joined the queue once again to buy yet another ticket, but a man in his forties, with his chubby son beside him eating candyfloss, nimbly slipped among the people and reached the till ahead of us.

During my eighty years in Naples, everyone has observed one very simple rule: never pick a fight with a fellow who is well built and covered with tattoos, and who speaks with a strong dialect. It isn't a city where you want to indulge in nitpicking. And yet I went over to this fellow and said, 'Excuse me, kind sir, have you noticed that there's a queue?'

He gave me a bored look and replied, 'Yep, I have.'

I saw red. 'Perhaps I didn't explain myself very well. You have to go to the back!'

At that moment I had his full attention. 'What do you want?' he said in a tone that was confidential but still far from friendly.

'You to go to the back!' I said vehemently.

A man behind me tugged me by the arm and whispered, 'Leave it be.'

If I had had time, I would have turned and raged at him too, even though he was just trying to save me. I would have slapped him in the face with the truth: that it's because everyone leaves things be that people around here go on being insolent. But I didn't have time, because the big guy seemed quite irritated by my words and was advancing threateningly towards me. I was about to turn myself into a retired colonel, and would have done so had it not been for the arrival of the security man, who handed the tickets to my interlocutor and, unbelievably, asked him to let it go. And he did: he let it go, like all the other people in Naples who are masters in letting things go, apart from yours truly. I would have liked to press the point, but Federico, standing beside me, was staring at me in terror, so I paid and we sat down in the coach for the umpteenth circuit.

A moment before the train set off, I turned towards my grandson and said, 'If you really want to live in this city, don't be like your grandad. Learn the sad and desperate art of "letting things go".'

I thought the amusement park would allow me to tick all the remaining empty boxes I hadn't filled for the function of grandfather, but when we left Federico demanded that we go to the zoo opposite, confirming my thesis that you should always give as little of yourself as possible in order to avoid creating excessive expectations in others. The fact was that after having absorbed pirates, spaceships, horses and dragons, I also had to witness the melancholy spectacle of animals in cages, another experience that I would happily have done without.

I learned that the flamingo owes its pink colour to the pigment of a microcrustacean on which it feeds, that only fifteen per cent of newborn ostriches reach their first year because of all the predators, and that black swans are monogamous and spend their whole lives with a single companion. It would be quite funny if we turned the same colour as the things we eat as well, and what a tragedy it would be if only a small percentage of babies reached adulthood. Imagine if human beings were monogamous and spent the whole of their lives with one single person. Only a few animals can do that.

Anyway, I came out of there satisfied that I had given my grandson a memory which might stay with him for the rest of his life. So I was walking along calmly and smugly with Federico beside me, when I bumped into my terrible neighbour. In fact, he was on the opposite pavement and hadn't noticed me. He had just emerged from a bank with two other people, with whom he was smiling and joking. Seeing him so calm and secure in his nice dark jacket, I doubted for a moment that he was the same person who had put Emma in that dreadful state. I stopped to watch those well-dressed individuals chattering and gesticulating, figures like any others and therefore invisible; three outlines which, if he hadn't been one of them, would have passed in front of my eyes for just a moment before being erased by the day, a bit like morning clouds.

At first glance there was nothing wrong with my neighbour: smartly dressed, clean and smiling face, reassuring appearance. However, the mere sight of him made me shiver. How can a man have two different appearances? How can he make sure that one doesn't contaminate the other? And why is evil so often imperceptible to other people? Perhaps because it's in the darkness that lies beneath the surface. Like clouds whose heads are lit by the rays of the sun while their bodies are filled with rage.

'Who is that?' Federico suddenly asked.

'A friend,' I said without hesitation.

I went on staring at the enemy until he noticed me. It was only then that the smile disappeared from his face. I'm not a coward – or at least, I fight every day not to be one – and yet at the sight of his predatory eyes I felt something very like fear. But then I told myself that he was the one who should be afraid of me rather than the other way round, so I held his gaze until the sleazeball turned away and vanished. After that I walked on, holding Federico by the hand.

'Aren't you going to say hello?' he asked.

'Another time,' I said.

Then I slipped into the nearest bar and made straight for the toilets. Another few moments and I would have disgraced myself.

Chapter Twenty-five

The Glass Bowl

Plates being shattered. A cry, then a thump. Another cry. I turn on the light, sit up on my mattress and wait. After a while I hear some more commotion, perhaps furniture being moved around and chairs dragged, then the sound of broken crockery. More shouting.

I get up and put on my clothes. I'm in the corridor when my neighbour's door opens. I hear running feet on the stairs, then hurry to the window. After a few seconds he comes out of the door and gets straight into his car. I run out on to the landing, where I find Eleonora Vitagliano waiting for me. She's motionless, and staring at Emma's half-open door.

'Did you hear that?' she whispers.

I nod. I haven't time to worry about the cat lady. I go over to the door and throw it open. Eleonora stands behind me.

'Eleonora, please!' I say, rather tactlessly.

She murmurs something and steps backwards. I ring the bell even though my hands are shaking more than usual. If this business doesn't end this evening, I swear I'm going to the police.

Emma doesn't reply. I should hurry inside, but I stay in the doorway. Something holds me back, and it isn't Signora Vitagliano, who is almost pushing me in with her eyes. I'm scared, and it's the real fear that you only feel a few times in your life, which paralyses your muscles and your thoughts. The problem is that at my age you can't afford to pay it too much heed, or you end up in an armchair studying the world from a distance, like Marino. So I push open the door and slip into the house.

The hallway is in darkness, the only light coming from a room at the end on the right. I want to run to it to check that Emma is all right, but my legs won't carry me, my head is spinning and my cataracts won't let me defeat the darkness. Then I calmly confront the corridor, my uncertain hands preceding my footsteps and opening up a path among the furniture.

Emma isn't in the kitchen. There are broken plates and glasses, an upturned chair, three open drawers. Then I notice red stains on the floor. Blood. The drops form a trail like Hansel and Gretel's breadcrumbs, showing me the way.

'Emma,' I whisper.

She doesn't reply.

God, I pray, let her be well. Let me die without witnessing yet another tragedy. I turn on the light in the corridor.

The trail of blood leads me to the bathroom. The towels are on the floor, like the soap dish, the toothbrush mug and the shower curtain. The drops have turned into prints left by bare feet.

I need a pee.

The cat lady's voice reaches me from the landing, but I can't make out her words. I feel as if I'm in a cotton-wool world, as if I've turned back into a foetus surrounded by amniotic fluid.

'Please,' I hear myself whispering, 'help me, as you've always done!'

But Caterina is far away, like the voice of Signora Vitagliano, like my children, like Rossana and Marino. They are far away from me and from everything that's happening here. The stench of shit can't reach them where they are.

Outside the bathroom there's an overturned washstand, and water and shards of glass on the floor. A little further on, a goldfish wiggles and gasps. *If I could, my friend, I would run and save you. I would put you in the basin and turn on the tap. No one should be denied their oxygen. I understand you – you have no idea how well I do – but I can't help you, not now.*

I'm sorry.

I turn around and step into the room opposite, the bedroom. The wardrobe doors are open, and there are some clothes scattered on the floor. On the mattress a half-full suitcase; at my feet a bloodstained shoe. My legs are about to give, and if they did I would slump on to the bed and not notice a hand protruding from behind it.

I don't know how I do it, but in a flash I'm kneeling beside Emma. Her eyes are open and she is panting. Blood is coming from her mouth, her face is swollen, one arm beneath her pelvis is in an unnatural position and a big pool of blood is spreading beneath the nape of her neck. All around her lie fragments of the wall mirror, giving a clear vision of the exact point where her head met the glass. Some streams of blood run thickly down the walls and trickle on to the floor, a few inches away from what remains of Emma.

You think you've seen everything in almost eighty years of life. You think you're prepared for every eventuality and that you can intervene with your experience, and instead you realize that you don't know anything – that the illnesses, the regrets and the traumas that have marked you didn't strengthen you in any way. You never learn how to confront grief – you go on living and that's that. As I am doing, without even being aware of it.

I take her hand and study her eyes.

She wants to speak, but she can't.

I look up. Eleonora is standing in the doorway, watching the scene with her mouth wide.

'Call the emergency services,' I tell her.

She doesn't move.

'Did you hear what I said?' I shout.

The cat lady nods and disappears from view.

'The ambulance is on its way, don't worry. You'll see, a few days and you'll be right as rain.'

There's a towel on the bed. I pick it up and place it under her head, trying to stop the haemorrhage. I don't know the right thing to do, but I act out of instinct; I have no time to reflect. I force myself to smile at her and not to look at the pool of blood that is spreading as far as the eye can see. Except that, as I have said, I'm not very good at pretending any more, and she must notice that, because she stares at me with clear eyes that seem to be begging me not to abandon her.

I know that look: it's the same as the one with which Caterina used to leave me speechless. So I struggle to open my mouth, even if I don't know what I'm saying. Life is giving me a second chance. It doesn't happen often.

'Don't think about anything. We're going to the hospital now. They will make you better, and a new journey will begin. I swear you will have what you deserve, even if it's the last thing that this foolish old man ever does!'

This time she smiles and gently clutches my hand. Her clotted blood makes our grip even firmer.

The cat lady appears in the doorway again and gives us a pitiful look. I nod and turn back towards Emma. I think the light is fading from her eyes.

'Do you know what I think, in fact? Once you've recovered, we'll take a little trip. I haven't moved for years. If you're well, of course. I understand that an old man's company isn't your highest aspiration, but you're going to have to get used to it, because I'm not going to let you go that easily!'

She smiles again. At least, it seems to me that she does. Or so I like to think. In fact, her grip is starting to weaken, and the towel is red and drenched through. I feel the need to cry and go to the bathroom. Another few minutes and I'm going to disgrace myself. So I go on chatting, waiting for the ambulance to come.

'But, I warn you, I'm not a great travelling companion. I'm lazy, I can't take a picture because my hands shake, my guts play up every now and again, and I can sometimes be cranky. But, you know, you've got to be patient with old people.'

This time I'm the only one smiling at my words. Signora Vitagliano has summoned the courage to step inside the room and look at us as if we were two ghosts. Emma is pale and it looks to me as if she's having a cold sweat. She's shivering. I take the sheet off the bed and cover her up, then approach her ear, a few inches from the dark pool that is inexorably continuing on its journey towards the skirting board. The blood scares us. Our bodies scare us – we find them dark and unknown, like space – and we try not to give too much weight to either, so as not to be crushed by them.

'You want to know a funny thing? A secret I've never told anyone?' I whisper. 'That Emma I was telling you about, the woman I was hopelessly in love with…'

Emma moves her pupils. So she is listening to what I'm saying.

'She was younger than you when I met her, and I never managed to win her. Don't look at me like that. I was married, but I've never told you I was a good man.'

The cat woman turns her head slightly to try and hear my words, but she's too deaf to pick up anything.

'However…I haven't told you the worst thing.'

I wait a few seconds. I thought I was going to take this secret with me to the grave, and instead I find myself confessing it to a girl I've only just met.

'Emma is my wife's sister…'

This time I'm sure she heard me. Her hand, however lightly, clenches around mine. Perhaps if she could Emma would call me a bastard; women show a lot of solidarity in these matters. That's why I've never talked about it to anyone, not even Rossana. Perhaps that's why I decided to do it now, to the only person who can't reply.

'In any case…' I try to go on, but at that moment two orderlies come into the room and shove me brusquely away from her.

I sit on the floor, watching Emma being helped by some individuals who move in unison and seem to know what they're doing. They don't talk to each other. One of them gets to work; the other checks her heartbeat, then her pupils. 'No, don't look at those eyes,' I want to shout. 'They're dark right now, but they'll come on again in a second. Please don't notice that Emma is dying.'

I try to get up, but I'm immediately forced to rest against the bed. The world is spinning around me. The two orderlies are still getting to grips with Emma; they take her arm from under her pelvis and rotate it. I decide that's too much. I leave the room and the flat and find myself on the landing, where the tenants have gathered in the meantime.

I hold up my hand to stop Marino, who is coming towards me, and walk over to the landing window, open it and throw up. A gust of fresh air strikes my face, and it's only then that I feel I can breathe again. A few feet down below, the light of a police car colours the faces of the few people standing down there looking up. I come back inside.

Emma is on a stretcher with her eyes closed. I don't ask any questions – I don't want to hear the answers.

Two policemen arrive, look around the place and then call for backup. One of the two of them stares at me. I think he might want to come over to me, but luckily the doctors distract his attention with a question.

'Are you coming with us?' they say, turning to me.

I nod; the police will have to wait. But they know it can't have been me – an old man hasn't the strength to do something so terrible. Insanity should wait for the third age to manifest itself – it would do a lot less damage.

I follow the stretcher. Emma isn't conscious any more.

Outside the bedroom my eye falls on the goldfish. It isn't wriggling any more; its suffering is over. Even in the life of a poor fish, luck counts for something – it happened to be in the wrong place at the wrong time. If it had ended up in my flat, right now it would be gliding calmly around in its bowl, at worst cursing the filthy conditions in which it was forced to spend its life.

No one is able to choose where their glass bowl will be placed – whether it is in the quiet kitchen of an old pensioner or on the side table in a house where a tragedy is about to be played out. It is chance, they say, that decides. And sometimes it can decree that our world will shatter into a thousand pieces and all we can do is gasp in the hope that some pious soul will pass by and pick us up.

The problem is that, in almost every case, the wait is longer than the death struggle.

Chapter Twenty-six

'The Fifth of May' from Memory

According to the clock it's twenty-one minutes past one. Last time I looked up the hands showed eighteen minutes past. Three minutes, and yet to me it has seemed like an eternity. The passageway is empty, my only company the hum of the coffee machine at the end of the corridor and the smell of alcohol floating in the air. She is inside – they've been operating on her for about two hours. Before closing the door in my face, a doctor took me aside and told me to expect the worst. I didn't have the strength to reply, and yet I should have done; I should have grabbed the doctor by the shirt and thrown him against the wall before shouting, 'Go away and save that girl's life. And don't try to tell me what to expect and what not!'

No one should take the trouble to tell other people what they should not expect from life. I expect Emma to come out with her eyes open; I expect her to look at me and smile, and then let me take her hand. I expect the child inside her to be able to emerge into this crazy world, and for that shitbag to be caught and thrown in a cell. I expect life not to make me witness another tragedy, perhaps the worst of all. I expect too many things already for a man I don't even know to dare to give me advice on what to expect.

I look at the blood-drenched cuff of my shirt, then turn back to the clock. How long is it going to take? How long do you need to save a girl's life? In whose hands does the responsibility lie? Who knows what those hands have been doing during the day. They will have gripped other hands, forks, napkins, maybe cigarettes, a pen, a steering wheel, a bar of soap, a book, a child's fingers, a scalpel.

Emma's parents should be out here, or some relative, at least some distant uncle, but I'm alone, as she was behind that door. We try to surround ourselves with people in the illusion that we will feel less exposed, but the truth is that you go into the operating theatre on your own. Just us and our bodies. Nothing more.

One thirty-one.

They say that when you get old you become selfish. I always have been, and yet now here I am, waiting for news of a woman I've only recently met, and who I thought I could help. Unfortunately life has taught me that no one can help anyone. We save ourselves on our own, if we want to.

I get up and walk towards the coffee machine. I shouldn't drink it, not at this time of night and at my age, but there are so many things that I shouldn't do – coffee isn't the first and it won't be the last. I down it in one gulp and go outside to smoke a cigarette. There are a few orderlies outside, talking in turn beside an ambulance. Hospitals are strange places, where joy is restrained so as not to cause too much annoyance to grief. On the floor above there is a happy girl with an infant on her breast, and in the operating theatre a woman of the same age fighting to keep hold of life. I take three puffs and go back to my seat. Sometimes one should switch one's brain off – another of those things we have no control over.

I hear footsteps. I look up and meet the distracted eye of a passing doctor. It's only when he's gone by that I realize he was the doctor who asked us lots of questions that evening. Luckily for him, he walks straight on and doesn't seem to recognize me, otherwise I would have had to explain what happened, and now one would find oneself having to sidestep a whole wagonload of regret. He, like me, could have avoided all that.

I get up again and go to the toilet. The mirror reflects my gaunt face, my glasses, my unkempt beard and Emma's blood all over me. After my heart attack the doctor told me I needed to take medicine, stop drinking, stop smoking, get regular sleep and avoid stress. In the course of three years I can confess that I violated four rules out of five, and only taking the medication stopped me from getting the full house. I would like to have that doctor in front of me now to ask him how he would abolish stress, if he knows a trick to manage that one.

For human beings anxiety is a physiological state; to get rid of it you would need to eliminate consciousness, as in the minds of babies and animals. I have a theory of my own about that. I maintain that things worked perfectly well until the creation of the monkey, after which something clogged the mechanism and out came man, a creature too intelligent for the tasks assigned to him. Intelligence is a precious quality. For us, however, it serves hardly any purpose except to invent stranger and stranger things that give us the illusion of being perfect. It doesn't help us understand why we are here; it doesn't make us less exposed than other creatures. It doesn't supply answers, but rather creates new questions. And too many questions increase unhappiness. I don't know if there are any living creatures apart from man who take their own lives, but if there are we're still the only ones who do it because we're weary of life. Why? Because whoever moulded us got the mixture of ingredients wrong, that's why.

But while we're on the subject of reckless theories, let's get back to doctors. I have to be honest, as a group they get on my nerves a bit. Not all of them, obviously, but most of them are walking on air most of the time. Saving a human life may give you a bit of a high, that much is true, but each of us should be able to bear in mind one small but crucial concept: we are moving around on a little ball that's rotating around a small yellow star like many others, in a tiny solar system in a peripheral zone of a little cigarette-shaped galaxy that moves majestically slowly. And there are still some people who waste their time feeling more important than the ants beside them.

I'm going mad – I wasn't made for waiting. If I spend too long staring at a wall, winged dragons start appearing, and two-headed harpies that feast on my unease in order to grow and leave the forced hibernation in which I normally keep them.

I need a beer.

It's damp outside and the streets are deserted. Luckily there's a bar still open just opposite the hospital; behind the bar there's a woman in her sixties, her hair dyed some months ago and held up with a hairband, a prominent belly and a grim expression on her face. I ask her for a beer. There, she's weighing me up: a decrepit old man having a lonely Peroni at two o'clock in the morning. In a squalid bar, I would add. Don't judge me, fat ugly woman who knows nothing about me. What, do you want me to judge your flabby arm with its tribal tattoo? It's a pathetic spectacle, but it's your own business – there must have been some reason why you decided to get a tattoo without thinking that your forearm would end up looking like a leg of pork.

I pay and leave. Vesuvius is still in front of me, with those

thousands of lights climbing almost to the top. They say
that in Naples wherever you turn you see the sea. In fact,
I think the volcano is a more imposing presence. It's there
wherever you happen to look. It's the two humps we look for
when we're trying to find our way home. It's the energy of
Vesuvius which, like lava, wedges itself among the buildings
and sets the alleyways alight.

I would happily stay here to enjoy the city at night,
slumbering placidly and contentedly, but I don't dare: I know
that at first light the creature will awaken, hungry again. So
I come back and sit back down on my chair.

One fifty-six.

I roll up my shirtsleeves and notice that my hands are still
trembling. I stop and stare at them and they seem so fragile,
with all those liver spots and all that wrinkled skin. Often,
when I look at myself in the mirror, I don't recognize myself.
Who knows why we always keep the best possible memory of
ourselves? Every time I see my body reflected, I almost feel
as if I'm looking at a bedraggled pair of pyjamas hanging in
the wind.

My phone rings: it's Marino's number. I should reply,
but I don't. What would I tell him? That I still don't know
anything and I've just had a beer?

After I'd been here for a while, two policemen came. One
of them, wearing a sickly sweet aftershave, came over to talk
to me.

'It was the husband,' I heard myself saying in a toneless
voice, 'but for now I'm waiting for Emma. I'll tell you everything afterwards.'

He looked at me. Perhaps he wanted to speak, perhaps
he could have forced me to give a statement, but instead
he nodded and walked away, letting the wake of aftershave
dissolve in a few seconds, drowned by the smell of alcohol.

The door at the end of the corridor is opening.

We're there. The moment has come to know the answer.

I jump to my feet and feel dizzy as my heartbeat quickens. The doctor stares at me; I stare back and walk uncertainly towards him. At my age I still haven't learned to manage my anxiety. In fact, there are lots of things that I haven't learned, and which no one has ever explained to me. They teach us equations, that poem by Manzoni, 'The Fifth of May', from memory, the names of the seven kings of Rome, but no one tells us how to confront our fears, how to accept our disappointments, where to find the courage to endure grief.

Chapter Twenty-seven

The Third of Three Unattainable Women

There's a big difference between the love for a woman you will never be able to have and the love for one you have. The first will shine for all eternity; the second will tend to go out, as the sun will in a few billion years. Both extinctions bring a lot of problems along with them. But we're talking about women, not stars, even if I think it would be easier to talk about the latter.

Emma is my wife's sister, a few years her junior. When I met Caterina, she was about twenty. At first I didn't notice her; as a boy you try to flirt with older women, to feel important. And at the end of the day that isn't so much of a mistake, because in fact you have your whole life to flirt with the younger ones.

So I fell in love with Emma gradually, one step at a time. When my passion for my wife began to diminish, I felt rage and disappointment. Rage towards myself, because I couldn't guard love; disappointment because the woman who no longer stirred my emotions was in my bed every night. So I decided to give her two children; at least they would lend a meaning to my loveless story of love. I know, it wasn't a fine gesture, but I'm sure many people know what I'm talking about.

Anyway, eventually the unexpected happened: Emma separated from her husband and Caterina invited her to move in with us for a while, to help her with her baby. She was twenty-six, I was nearly forty, and yet at that time I felt as if I were a boy again. My wife had already set her jaw to parry the blows of life, while Emma was still running along with her mouth open. Her expression and her body emanated life and lightness, sensations that had been alien to me for some time, and I was enraptured by so much radiance. The desire for youth is contagious; if it's all around you, you can't do without it. Some men change family, wardrobe and house just in exchange for a drop of vitality and a few years of thoughtless adolescence. I didn't change family, house or wife. My love for Emma was platonic, and yet it remains one of the most intense relationships in my life – confirmation that the more unrealizable a desire is, the more ceaselessly it burns.

Emma and I allowed ourselves to be dragged into a sinful vortex made of stolen glances, brushing hands and hugs that were never too intense. It takes a lot of patience and little courage to spend a life beside a woman that you don't love, particularly if the one you desire is in the next room. In any case, Emma left after a few months and the house was suddenly empty and silent. I tried to forget her and that time in our lives, but Caterina was always there to talk to me about her. One evening – I remember Caterina was rubbing cream on her hands – she told me her sister had fallen for her son's skiing instructor, and that she was going to spend the summer with him in Trentino. That night I didn't sleep a wink; I imagined Emma in the arms of a muscular man with a tanned and wrinkled face, whose breath smelled of grappa. It was a cliché, I admit, but in truth the very fact of going out with the skiing instructor is a prime cliché in itself. And yet she really did go to the mountains and she stayed there for two months. By the time she came back, however, her intense love affair was over: the skiing instructor had worked out that a young mother is more dangerous than a black-ice ski run, and chose to take another route.

That autumn Emma often came to our place for dinner, so that our children were together. I can't express the sensation that assailed me every time I turned round and noticed that she was staring at me. She immediately averted her eyes, and my only option was to stare at her profile like an idiot, waiting in vain for her to find the courage to meet my eye again.

Emma had everything that Caterina had lost along the way: the soft skin, the intoxicating smile and the seductive gaze. How could I resist them? And, in fact, one evening I lost control and went somewhere I had never gone before, under cover of a blanket. We were sitting on the sofa, Emma, Caterina and me, watching a film. The children were already asleep. To cut a long story short – it must have been because of the boring film – eventually I noticed her fingers a few inches away from mine, and I performed that most adolescent of gestures, holding her hand. It took me twenty minutes to seize hold of it, as if I were a snail struggling to drag its shell along. In the end Emma turned around and looked at me in shock. I should have stopped, but instead I exchanged her glance and didn't withdraw my hand. We stayed there like that, like a pair of lovers giving a start as they discover each other's body, more concentrated on the slightest movement of a thumb than on the plot of the film.

Caterina, sitting beside me, didn't notice a thing. Or perhaps she was kind enough to let me believe that. In any case, it was the most intimate gesture that ever bound me to Emma.

After that evening she became evasive, she steered clear of me, and if she was obliged to address me she did it without looking me in the eye. She felt it was her fault. It was quite normal – anyone in her place would have been in a state of torment. Anyone but me. At the time I didn't know that anomalous feeling that would pay me a visit much later. For years I piled up worries and regrets in a corner; obviously sooner or later the construction was going to come tumbling down.

I waited a few months before resolving the situation. It was Christmas Day, and the whole family was sitting around the table. Emma was on the other side from me. The days of complicit glances seemed to be over, so much so that I started to feel awkward in her presence, uncertain about her real desire for me. Perhaps I had been deceiving myself, or I had misinterpreted some of her attitudes; perhaps my boundless self-esteem had made me take a step too far. And yet, when she got up to go to the kitchen I made an excuse to follow her. Luckily the voices that reached me from the dining room protected me against possible intrusions.

Emma had her back to me. I put my arms around her hips and said, 'I know it would be crazy, but you know me – I get bored of routines!'

It certainly wasn't what you would call a great declaration of love, and yet she laughed, perhaps because she had got to know me. But after two seconds she turned serious again, looked me in the eye and said, 'Cesare, you're mad, you know that? This has to stop!'

'It hasn't begun…'

She sighed and lowered her head. I remember that, for a moment, I thought of kissing her, but a moment later she cut me short.

'Why did you have two children with her if you don't love her?'

A million-dollar question. I should have sat down and lit a cigarette and talked for hours about the fact that to live a life that's really worth living you need to take important decisions every morning. Unfortunately I find making choices absolutely terrifying, and I've never done it. That's why I have been incomplete as a person.

Obviously I said something quite different: 'We're talking about us, not Caterina.'

At that point she burst out: 'Caterina is my sister, but apparently that doesn't matter to you!'

I put my hand over her mouth to keep her angry tone from reaching the dining room. Emma didn't pull away, so I found the courage to stroke her neck. It was an act of pure madness, I have to admit. She could have slapped me and run from the room. And I don't know how I would have made it back to the table. Instead I let my fingers brush her soft skin before half closing my eyes. Then I thought, *Well, Cesare, you've got to kiss her now.* And I swear I would have done if my nephew hadn't fallen from his tricycle at that very moment, burst into tears and started calling for his mother like a mad thing. Two seconds later, Emma was back in the dining room and the moment had vanished into nothing.

That evening I found a piece of paper in my jacket pocket. It said: *We can't.*

Even today I find myself thinking about that fateful episode. Perhaps destiny had a hand in it. I should be grateful to my nephew who, by falling, managed to steal a memory that might have made me ashamed. Instead I think he only added one more regret to my already impressive collection.

Emma had another two serious relationships over the years. For a long time I only met her at family parties. She never even gave me one of those looks that made me shiver. Some years later, her sister persuaded her that we should all spend the summer together. What has stayed with me of that time is the house overlooking the sea, the smell of the embers at night, the incessant song of the crickets in the silence of the night, the creak of the door leading to the garden, the cries of the gulls in the early morning, Emma's wet hair dripping on her shoulders when she came back from the sea. Ten years had passed since I had started to look at her differently, and her beauty had, if possible, evolved.

Never did I desire her so much with my whole being as I did that summer. But she didn't give me a way of flirting with her; whenever she noticed that I was looking at her she made some excuse to leave and ran off to hug her companion, a very nice accountant who admitted a few years later that he had been gay all along. When I found out, I wanted to run to his house and beat him up. *So here I am drooling after her for a lifetime while you share her bed every night, and then you have the nerve to come out as gay?* Either way, towards the end of the holiday, Emma yielded and returned my complicit glance. Then, one afternoon, when everyone in the house was asleep, I joined her in the sea. I dived in, and with a few strokes I was by her side.

She seemed to turn pale, but she said nothing. I can still see the desire to kiss me written on her face. Instead, after a while, she said, 'Cesare, maybe it's all a big game to you. But you want to know one thing? It isn't for me. I've always been in love with you, since the first time you looked at me. I've been avoiding you for ten years, and I have no intention of giving in now!'

I froze. It's one thing to hope that a woman who is driving you mad shares the sentiment, quite another to know for certain.

'It isn't a game to me,' I said seriously.

'Then what is it?'

I approached her mouth, as her eyes wandered from my lips to my eyes. I would have kissed her, then confessed once and for all that I loved her, perhaps even revealed that I wanted to leave her sister. Instead I was interrupted by the arrival of Sveva, who would have been about twelve at the time. I heard her voice behind me and my heart leapt into my mouth. She was swimming with some friends, a few yards away, and looking at me with puzzlement, trying to interpret the strange scene she had just witnessed.

Emma flushed and fell backwards, while I plunged under the water and stayed there for a few seconds, long enough to recover from the shock and invent a plausible excuse.

'Darling,' I said at last when I re-emerged.

'What are you doing?'

'Nothing. Your aunt was telling me something. Nothing important,' I said with a half-witted smile.

Emma was quicker. She went over to her niece and whispered in her ear, 'Your father's a great gossip – he always wants to know what other people are up to!'

My daughter looked at us, then decided just to giggle. From then onwards Sveva never mentioned the incident, but I know she knows, and that sooner or later she will throw it in my face. However, that was the last time I found myself an inch away from kissing Emma.

When Caterina died many years later, Emma hugged me for a long time, as she had never done in the past, and murmured in my ear, 'Thank me, because now you'd have had a fine regret to live with!'

I said nothing. I should have recanted right there, by my wife's deathbed.

My regret, my dear Emma, is here with me and wakes me every morning. And you know what it whispers to me? You chain yourself to something or someone every time you don't make a choice.

Chapter Twenty-eight

Unforeseen Hypothesis

Naples at dawn looks elegant and austere. The empty streets, the parked cars lying silently with salt on their windows, the cries of gulls in the distance, the deafening noise of a shutter coming up, the smell of brioches wafting among the alleys, the clink of coffee cups from the few bars that have already opened. You don't hear voices, chatter, laughter, and those few human beings wandering around the streets seem to respect the solemnity of the moment. Perhaps the city knows that Emma is dead and tonight this poor old tottering man has just had the umpteenth blow in his life. Naples respects other people's pain because it knows what it's talking about.

I need a coffee. I go into a cafe and cling to the bar. The barista gives me a curious look before serving me. I must look pale as a ghost. If Sveva knew how I spent the night she would give me one of her lectures. But, in fact, this time it isn't my fault. I just did what anyone would have done in my position: try to save the life of an innocent young woman.

The police told me they had collared her husband, who was wandering the streets in a confused state. It's strange, but I can't feel angry about him. Emma's death has set my emotions back to zero, so much so that even weeping seems impossible.

I knew as soon as I saw the doctor coming towards me: his face promised nothing good. And yet I still hoped there might be a small possibility, that Emma was in a coma, but perhaps they could wake her up. If you look death in the face, you understand that all the things people say about dying, like 'I'd rather die than spend the rest of my life in a wheelchair', are so much nonsense. When the moment comes to choose, you're ready to barter anything just to stay alive. But for Emma there was nothing left to barter with. She passed away after fighting for a whole night, taking with her the child that she was guarding.

The doctor told me she'd had a haemorrhage in her head and another in her abdomen, her pelvis and one arm were fractured, and the bones in her face were shattered. As if she'd been run over by a tractor. How much hatred do you need to commit such carnage? How is it possible for a man like that to live a normal life? And for no one ever to have noticed anything? Still, it isn't enough to guess – you need to act. But action needs something that not everyone possesses: courage. So I've never done much for other people, or indeed for me. In fact, to change a life, whether it's your own or the life of someone dear to you, you need a generous supply of audacity. That's the whole problem.

My hands are shaking more than usual, and even bringing the cup to my lips seems like a huge enterprise. The barista gives me a compassionate look. If it were an ordinary day I would give him a suitable reply. Other people's pity makes me furious. But today isn't an ordinary day. And yet, looking around, you would think it was. Life goes on, heedless of the pieces it leaves along the way.

I should have reported that bastard and really saved Emma rather than wasting time on letters that were as stupid as they were pointless. But she didn't want me to get involved. She thought she could get by on her own; she was ashamed of her situation. Who can say what mechanism had installed itself within her? Who can say why abused women feel ashamed about themselves and their partners? There's something absurdly perverse in the fact that one part of Emma wanted to shield her tormentor from the judgement of others.

My head is spinning and I need to sleep. But first I decide to have the barista wrap the last two *sfogliatelle*, the sweet ricotta puffs, from behind the bar. Marino is mad about them. Then I hail a cab and, for once, I say nothing until I get home.

Emma's door is sealed with tape and the landing no longer seems familiar to me. Even my flat feels alien. Or perhaps I'm just looking at it in a different way. There isn't even any sign of Beelzebub, perhaps because he knows there's a bad feeling around here. He is the perfect embodiment of egoism – not like me, trying to convince myself every day that even if the world around me were collapsing I would keep going straight on along my chosen path. Well, the world really collapsed today and I don't think I've carried straight on without turning around.

I put the package of pastries on the kitchen table and slump on to the sofa. The cup Emma used is still beside me. I avert my eyes and look at Leo Perotti's painting. How lovely to be a comic-book character, a stereotype, someone who already knows what he needs to do and how to do it. Superman knows that he will spend his whole life fighting evil. There's some sense in that – at least he won't waste his time trying to find his way.

Perhaps now I should really go to bed. I have no tears to shed, just crazy thoughts like the desire, for example, to go to sleep and wake up again in three months. People confronting an obstacle take a run and jump over it, while I do the clever thing and walk past it. In a word, I don't know how to confront the moment. I thought I'd seen everything, but I hadn't.

The phone rings. It's eight in the morning. I exhale noisily and go to answer it, extremely slowly. This morning even the simplest movements feel like an unclimbable mountain. As soon as I pick up, I hear Marino's voice.

'Cesare, at last! I've been trying to call you all night! How are you?'

I'd like to stop the conversation right there. Only Marino could think of asking such a question at that moment.

'How do you think I am?' I say irritably.

I should really tell him that my eyes are closing, my legs are shaking, I'm breathless and my stomach is starting to hurt. But I'm not used to complaining. In my place, Marino would have complained already.

'I have no words for what happened…' he says after a while.

'Right,' I say.

There really are no words.

'I'm sorry. Perhaps it was my fault we wasted our time. If I'd known how to print…'

I can't help smiling at the thought of that shabby letter.

'Marino, it's not our fault.'

'Yes, I know,' he says, 'but maybe we could have done something.'

His voice is breaking with emotion. Damn it all, I'm trying not to cry, then he comes along and does it in my place. Next time I'll have to get in ahead of him.

'Marino, she couldn't have been saved. That's the truth!'

He stops talking.

I ruminate on my words. I know they're clumsy, particularly right now, but they represent what I'm thinking. Part of Emma wanted help. The other part hoped she wouldn't get it.

'What do you mean?'

'The bastards who hit women do it because they know they can get away with it. Emma didn't love herself, and at first she almost thought it was normal to be abused. She basically thought nothing had happened. She thought she deserved it!'

Marino doesn't reply.

'You know one thing? Her father beat her...' I add a moment later.

But the old man still doesn't say anything.

'There are various guilty parties in this horrible story,' I say at last. 'But we certainly aren't among them!'

He waits for a few seconds before breaking the silence. 'Do you want me to come up to yours for a bit?' he asks.

I would really like to get some sleep, but I know it would be impossible, so I tell him that'll be fine. I'll wait for him and give him his pastry – that might be enough to make him feel less wretched.

I come back to the kitchen, open yet another beer and light another cigarette. The pain in my stomach has got worse, and now I'm feeling a pain in my chest as well. I walk towards the sitting room and notice the half-open door of the box room, and remember the romper suit. I furiously take the lid off the box and find that it's still there. I pick it up and bring it to my nose. It smells good, as if it's already had a baby inside it. A tear slips down my face, unnoticed. Strange how, over the past few days, the storeroom seems

to have become a therapist's consulting room – it's the only place where I can give vent to my grief. I should throw the rompers in the bin – what use will they be to me except to remind me of these terrible events for ever? Instead I put them back in their place and close the box.

I try to get back to the sofa, even though I don't think I can even stay upright. In the dining room I feel a stitch in my chest. I stretch my arm out towards the doorpost, almost as if to check whether my premonition was correct.

Everything is silent.

I relax my hold and slide towards my goal. Another stitch, very powerful this time, crushes my chest. My cigarette falls from my lips as the bottle of Peroni slips from my hand and smashes to the ground. I would like to cry out, but my voice suffocates in my throat, my legs go and I drop to the floor, into the beer that mingles with the urine that is now beginning to wet my trousers.

I'm dying: I've had some experience of heart attacks. But this one seems more painful than before. If I weren't an atheist, I would think it was the right time to go. I might even deceive myself that there is a meaning, that perhaps God is calling me to help Emma, as if I were somehow knowledgeable about what awaits us on the other side. The Lord is using me to help a poor girl, granting me the possibility of again trying to save her. If I were a believer, I would die happy. Instead I'm furious: Emma and I bite the dust while the monster who killed her is still around. It doesn't strike me as fair, but basically justice is a concept invented by man – it doesn't exist in nature.

I try to shout, even though no one can hear me, but all that comes out of my mouth is a rattle, not unlike Beelzebub's purrs when he patiently waits to be served some ham. My eyes are closed and yet I can still see him, Signora

Vitagliano's cat, looking at me from the sitting-room door as if I were an old piece of furniture that can be safely ignored. I stretch out my hand; for the first time I'm the one who needs him. '*Go and get help,*' I want to say to him. The cat looks at me for a moment, then gets bored, brings his paw to his mouth and devotes himself to a washing session. I'm dying; he's washing himself. It's like a joke: lived like an egoist, died because of an egoist. Life has decided to teach me a lesson.

I close my eyes and give up. The doctor always told me not to do it; told me to lead a regular life, not to smoke, not to take the blue pill with Rossana, not to drink. *Too many prohibitions, doctor, and life becomes a millstone.* And this way Sveva will be able to draw her own conclusions, everyone will be able to think that she warned me and she will have one regret less to live with. She might even laugh with her brother and their friends over dinner as they reminisce about my proverbial pig-headedness. Maybe Rossana will cry. Marino will, though, not least because he will be the one who finds me.

I'm starting to feel cold. I've always thought that heart attacks were one of the best ways to go. No years of suffering, therapy, hospitals, people giving you pitying looks, or hiding the truth from you; a quick blow and 'bye then'. Instead I've been on the floor for at least three minutes, pondering existence while the screen goes dark. An unforeseen hypothesis. My life has been full of unforeseen hypotheses.

Beelzebub comes over and starts licking my cheek. If I had the strength I would punch that bloody cat right in the head. Instead I decide to relax and yield to sleep. Now I don't feel any pain, just weariness.

Marino has the keys to my flat – he could save me. But will he work out what's happened? And, more importantly, how long will it take him to go downstairs and come back? My salvation is in the hands of a foolish old man with the reflexes of a sloth.

Bye, world. It's been nice knowing you, even if you really are a total bastard!

Chapter Twenty-nine

I Like

'You know what I'd like to eat right now?' I whisper in Sveva's ear as she bends over me.

She looks at me as she looks at her son. 'Dad, stop it,' she says.

'A bit of prosciutto crudo,' I continue.

Of all the food that could have come to mind, I chose ham. The older you get, the more you lose your sweet tooth. In every respect.

'I'd like you to bring me a nice packet of thin-cut prosciutto, the kind that almost melts in your mouth.'

My mouth is watering; in fact, there are days when I eat nothing but slops.

Dante, Leo and Rossana laugh; Sveva gets irritated. I don't know if I've already mentioned this, but my daughter has no sense of humour.

It was Marino who saved me from death. Almost unbelievably, he came upstairs with the front door keys, and when he saw that I wasn't opening up he came in. When anyone asked him to explain, he said he thought it seemed normal to bring the keys, just in case I'd dozed off on the sofa. He saved my life, although not all by himself.

When I got to hospital, I found out later, I was more that

side than this, and they had to keep me in intensive care for three days. I'm better now, but I'll have to have an operation if I want to go on acting the fool for another few years. In ten minutes they're going to come and take me to the operating theatre, then they'll open up my chest and try to adjust my ailing heart. It's funny to think of it: perfect strangers are struggling, sweating, shouting, cursing to save my skin, and I just lie there sleeping as if the problem weren't mine. One of the rare cases in which man entrusts his own life to one of his fellows. Otherwise, we always think about trying to do things better than other people.

But I'm not very frightened. Perhaps because I've worked out that dying is really like getting a suntan: you can't keep your eyes open. That's it.

'When you get home, you'll have that packet of prosciutto!' Sveva says, her eyes glistening.

'Don't cry, little one. I'm not very sure they want me up there. I'm a rotten neighbour!'

When I say the word 'neighbour', Emma comes back into my mind. I don't think I was a bad neighbour to her. I would like to be able to ask her; it would let me swallow the lump of tar that's been stuck in my throat since that horrible night. The doctors say it's because of the intubation, but I know that's not true; it's the feeling of guilt that I still can't digest, and which rises up inside me like an acid reflux. *I did what I could, Emma. I hope you understood that.*

'How can you be so frosty and facetious, even at a time like this?' Sveva asks. 'Sometimes I wish I was more like you. Instead I think I've picked up only your shortcomings.'

'Well, you have to get old before you can laugh at life. At my age you'll be adorable!'

Maybe it's a way of staving off the fear of leaving the operating theatre feet first, but I think I can't help being facetious. There are two ways of confronting things, with despair and with irony, and neither of these changes the cards on the table. We can't decide the final result, but we can choose how we're going to spend the last five minutes.

'Idiot!' Sveva says and taps me on the arm.

Rossana joins in: 'The truth is that he can't help being the centre of attention. The old boy's pretty pleased with himself!'

This time I do the smiling. If I get through this, I'll have to set myself the objective of persuading Rossana to retire from her work and tend only to me. I think I'll have a tough job, but at least it will keep me busy. Dante told me she'd been praying for two whole days outside the intensive-care ward.

Marino didn't make it in, but he did phone once an hour and wept like a baby the first time I answered. The usual good old heart of steel.

My son is leaning on the edge of the bed. I'd like to push him further away – his aftershave is making me ill – but, damn it, I've done so much to get close to him, I can't ruin everything right now.

'Listen, I know it's not the moment, but we've got to find a solution after the operation. You either come to mine or to Sveva's. You can't stay on your own!'

Good God, not at Sveva's. But my son's place doesn't seem like a great idea either. I don't dare to imagine the spectacle of him and his artist in their dressing gowns holding hands on the sofa. I should tell him the truth, but he's so gentle that I can't reply. Dante, unlike his sister, knows how to deal with me. So I nod; I'm not up to talking about things right now. One problem at a time. First I've got to get through this, then I'll work out which of my children I want to ruin what's left of my days with.

In fact, there's another possibility: staying at home with a carer, as long as she's not too old. But I can't even say that: Rossana is sitting right next to me, and it wouldn't sound that great a joke. And then I've got one small niggle: if I get through this today, it'll be time to say goodbye to my old friend down there. Without the little blue pill it's retirement time. That should be normal at my age, but it isn't. It's sad to think that a friend you've been so bound to, and who has never betrayed you, suddenly says goodbye. A bloody nuisance, I don't need to say. At this point in life you begin to lose your eyesight as well, so at least I won't be forced to watch a spectacle I don't know what to do with.

In come two nurses. It's time to get going.

Now Dante seems moved as well, and Sveva has turned away.

'Hey, kids, I'm not dead yet!' I manage to say before Dante hugs me.

I'm not really cut out for tear-jerking scenes. If I really had to die, I'd rather do it in my sitting room, with Beelzebub licking my cheek. At least I wouldn't have had time to get emotional.

One of the two orderlies has to inject something into my drip, so he unhooks the bed and then drags me out into the corridor. The fluorescent lights on the ceiling follow me along my journey. I should close my eyes – there's nothing nice to look at here. But if I'm going to be dead soon I don't want to throw away the chance to gaze upon the last things of this world, even if they are nothing but plain white fluorescent lights.

The first person I saw after recovering from my heart attack was my grandson, who stroked what hair I still have left. I was already nervous, I didn't remember anything and I only wanted to go home. I don't like hospitals and the very thought of having to stay there for any amount of time was depressing. Then, however, Signora Filomena came to change my drip…and the world smiled at me again. She's a nurse in her fifties, curvaceous, tanned, raven hair, a lot of make-up, lipstick – and a glorious pair on her! New York has its symbolic Statue of Liberty; we, thanks to Signora Filomena, can respond with our own statue of vulgarity, as long as it bears her features. But, in fact, the nurse has made me cocky again: I like them pretty rough.

The next day I called her and asked her to adjust my pillows. Then I lay there with an idiotic look on my face, enjoying her bosoms an inch away from my nose, as she fiddled around to make me comfortable.

In the end, she smiled and said, 'Well, sir, we are a one, aren't we!'

Yes, I do like to be a one. I like to be facetious, to not take life too seriously. I like pretty, voluptuous women. But I like lots of other things as well. For example, I like the smell of cooking that reaches me through an open window, or the curtain in the summer, stirred by a gust of wind. I like dogs that lean their head on one side to listen to you, or houses that have recently been whitewashed. I like it when a book is waiting for me on the chest of drawers. I like jam jars and the yellow glow of street lamps. I like the feel of raw meat and fish. I like the sound of a bottle being uncorked. I like the red wine that clings to the glass. I like old fishing boats with their paint flaking. I like familiar places and the smell of laundries. I like cork floats and butchers slicing meat with regular movements. I like red cheeks and a quaver in the voice.

We're in the lift. One orderly pushes me; the other one presses the button. Here too the light is white and aseptic. I'm aware of anxiety rising from my guts and swelling in my chest. I close my eyes and go on listing things.

I like the smell of newborn babies and the distant playing of a piano. I like the sounds of feet on gravel and paths that twist like streams through the fields. I like Vesuvius, which makes me feel at home. I like sinking my feet into the sand. I like Sunday afternoon football, the smell of a new bar of soap, fogged windows on cold days. I like it when a woman says 'I love you' with her eyes. I like the crackle of chestnuts on the embers. I like the silence of summer evenings and the sound of the waves at night. I like the sound of chirruping outside the window, the water that bathes your feet and the bark of an old olive tree under your fingertips. I like the smell of chimneys as I walk along the cobblestones of a mountain village. I like home-made pasta and writing on walls. I like the smell of dung in a wet field. I like wooden spoons. I like the cactus that knows how to adapt, and the sound of a hidden stream. I like the anchovy fritters sold in front of Dante's gallery.

Another corridor to go down; it feels as if it will never end. The two orderlies beside me greet their colleagues, chat and joke. For them I'm just another body on its way to the slaughter, just a part of the daily routine. If you look at death beside you every day, after a while you can't help yawning.

I like the bubbling of the coffee pot on the gas, the stones polished by the sea and the sound of dishes in a restaurant. I like a cat wandering furtively among the cars and the creak of old furniture. I like a wave in the distance and the curious expression of tourists looking at my city. I like tree-lined avenues. I like the smell of old grocery shops that no longer exist. I like people playing music in the street. I like the colour of tomatoes and the smell of cream on bodies. I like summer afternoons accompanied by the song of crickets. I like taking a strand of spaghetti from the boiling water and biting it. I like the smell of fish in a rusty old fishing boat, and the moon painting the wake in the water to reach it. I like photographs that allow you to travel through time. I like the squeak of wooden floors. I like shortcomings. I like an old ruin in a wheat field. I like to look down on a beach carpeted with a thousand umbrellas of different colours. I like old songs that take your breath away. I like crabs scuttling away into the hollow of a rock. I like the goal drawn on an unplastered wall for a game of football. I like feeling a woman's hand on the back of my neck.

The two orderlies take the edges of the blanket and lift me up. A moment later I'm on the bed in the operating theatre. My heart is beginning to pump more quickly. I try to relax and not think about what will happen in a few minutes. Two doctors come, one holding a file. The other one takes my arm. I close my eyes again. I don't want to see anything any more; I just want to imagine.

I like birds that take shelter under a gable and wait for the rain to stop. I like the city sleeping, and the sight of a bucket and spade set down on the sand. I like the snail dragging itself energetically to a hiding place. I like bicycle bells. I like the lizards that don't run away but stay motionless. I like the crosses on mountain peaks. I like the white of seaside houses and old courtyards with the clothes hung out to dry. I like it when a memory seeks me out. I like the wind that moves obstacles aside and the ripe fruit abandoning the branches. I like the ants that drink from a drop of dew. I like a little field on the edge of town. I like the roads that lead to the sea. I like walking barefoot in the summer. I like faces wrinkled by life. I like a man working in the fields in the distance. I like people who love a child that isn't their own.

The doctor with a mask over his mouth pats my arm and then asks, 'Signor Annunziata, is everything all right?'

You're about to open me up like a watermelon, I don't know if I'm going to survive the operation, and you ask me if everything's all right? I nod to keep from cursing, as I feel someone fiddling about with a needle in my vein, then I become aware of the cold metal on the skin of my ankles and wrists. The smell of alcohol is everywhere, and I don't like the smell of alcohol.

But I do like the smell of lemon that sticks to your fingers, and the smell of dark earth that slips beneath your finger-nails. I like the smell of pines and the aroma of freshly washed laundry. I like the rattle of hail on windowpanes and the texture of volcanic rock. I like the gradually fading smell of coffee and the smell of melting chocolate that arrives a little later. I like wooden beams in a ceiling, breadcrumbs and objects that no one uses any more. I like meeting the eye of a woman I don't know. I like the secure movements of a pizza-maker, hugs of elation, the hand of an infant reaching into the air. I like ivy climbing over the facade of a building. I like fish nibbling at bread on the surface of the water and darting away. I like people reading at bus stops. I like people who don't plan too much and are good at being on their own. I like cooking on a veranda. I like the smell of sweat after a long run. I like people who always see the glass as half full. I like white hair and the wooden scales that greengrocers used to use. I like houses that welcome you with the smell of cooking. I like the smack of lips on skin. I like those who love first.

Some lights go out. The doctor leans over my face and, in a reassuring voice, says, 'Signor Annunziata, we're going to make you sleep now. You will wake up in your room when we've finished. Don't worry, it'll all be fine!'

I don't even open my eyes. I will wake up in my room. Or I won't. Subtle difference.

I like the light in the sky when the sun has gone down. I like the grass that defeats the tarmac. I like the daft smile of a clown. I like people who don't bear grudges. I like an untidy old bookshop. I like the moment before the first kiss. I like looking at the buildings in an unknown city. I like the dignity of a son carrying his old mother behind the hearse. I like women who like food. I like reading a book in the shade. I like geckos who study the horizon from their spot beside a lamp. I like those with the strength to believe in something with all their heart. I like swallows' nests. I like people who are still astonished by the stars. I like the smell of walls and glowing coals that welcome the loves of a single summer. I like the hum of a fan in the background. I like imagining the face of a woman seen from behind. I like bales of hay in the fields beside the road. I like people who know how to ask for forgiveness. I like people who haven't yet worked out how to find their way in the world. I like people who know how to ask. I like my children's smiles.

I like people who know how to love one another.

Nothing else comes to mind – perhaps the anaesthetic has already entered my bloodstream? Better to sleep – I'll resume the list later.

Oh, wait, I've got one last *I like*.

I like people who fight every day to be happy.

Acknowledgements

I'd like to thank some people.

First of all my wife Flavia, who was there when I was struggling to find my way and who is still there now. Still smiling.

Then I would like to thank Silvia Meucci, my agent and friend, the first to notice me, to hold out her hand and lead me here. The fact that this book exists is to a large extent down to her.

Thanks to my editor at Longanesi, Stefano Mauri, who has not missed an opportunity to speak well of me and Cesare.

My thanks to Giuseppe Strazzeri, the publishing director, one of those people who has the ability to make you feel at ease. The enthusiasm and commitment that he has given to Cesare have been his lifeblood.

Thanks to Guglielmo Cutolo: apart from being a great editor, in many respects he speaks my language. His precious work improved the novel.

Heartfelt thanks, last of all, to the whole Longanesi family, which welcomed me with solicitude, affection and friendship, making me feel part of the household.

Oneworld, Many Voices

Bringing you exceptional writing from around the world